THE WORLD OF
NORM
INCLUDES DELIVERY

ORCHARD BOOKS

First published in Great Britain in 2016 by The Watts Publishing Group

1 3 5 7 9 10 8 6 4 2

Text © Jonathan Meres 2016
Illustrations © Donough O'Malley 2016

A CIP catalogue record for this book
is available from the British Library.

ISBN 978 1 40834 193 3

Printed and bound in Great Britain by CPI Group (UK) Ltd, Croydon, CR0 4YY

The paper and board used in this book are from well-managed forests
and other responsible sources.

MIX
Paper from
responsible sources
FSC® C104740

Orchard Books
An imprint of

Hachette Children's Group
Part of The Watts Publishing Group Limited
Carmelite House
50 Victoria Embankment
London EC4Y 0DZ
An Hachette UK Company
www.hachette.co.uk
www.hachettechildrens.co.uk

JONATHAN MERES

THE WORLD OF NORM

INCLUDES DELIVERY

ORCHARD

To Inigo Armand Valentin Albini Ben LeBlanc.
Because ... well, just because.

CHAPTER 1

Norm knew it was going to be one of those days when he lost his house. Or rather, when he mistook someone **else**'s house for his own. But it amounted to the same thing. Getting one house mixed up with another. Which was easily done. Well, if you were Norm it was easily done, anyway. And Norm **was** Norm.

In his defence, though, Norm wasn't particularly observant at the best of times, let alone when he'd been dawdling back from school, head in the clouds, daydreaming of the weekend ahead

and how he intended spending as much of it as possible on his bike. Norm tended **not** to notice things. Like the time he **didn't** notice that the toilet wasn't where it normally was and he ended up nearly peeing in his dad's wardrobe. Or the time he failed to notice that he'd just brushed his teeth with mayonnaise instead of toothpaste. Quite why the mayonnaise had been in the bathroom to start with was another

matter entirely. That wasn't the point. The point was that in the unlikely event of there ever being a world championship for **noticing** things, Norm

6

definitely wouldn't win any medals. Assuming, of course, that Norm had even noticed that there actually **was** a world championship for noticing things, in the first place. Which was even unlikelier. But that wasn't the point either. The point was that Norm was spectacularly rubbish when it came to noticing things. Like which house he lived in, for instance.

Then again, it still wasn't **all** that long since they'd moved from their **old** house. Or rather, it still wasn't all that long since they'd **had** to move from their old house because his dad had been fired and they'd had to start eating supermarket own-brand Coco Pops instead of **proper** Coco Pops. So Norm could **almost** be forgiven for getting mixed up. Not that it was an actual **crime** to mistake another house for your own. But it was **definitely** a crime to try and break in. Not that Norm was **aware** that he **was** trying to break in, of course. As far as he was concerned he was just trying to open the flipping front door. His **own** flipping front door.

"What do you think you're **doing**?" said a voice.

"Uh?" said Norm, turning around and coming face to face with the owner of the voice. And she didn't look too happy, either. Quite the opposite, in fact.

"I said, what do you think you're **doing**?"

Norm was confused. Firstly, because the door was refusing to open. And, as far as he knew, his mum and dad hadn't suddenly decided to move house again and not bother telling him. Although, frankly, he wouldn't put it past them. Secondly, because there was a strange woman standing in front of him, pulling a face like a cat's backside.

"Sorry, do I know you?" said Norm.

"I **could** ask you the same question!" said the woman.

What? thought Norm. **He** could ask **her** all **kinds** of flipping questions if he wanted to. Like, how come she was looking at him like he was something she'd just scraped off the bottom of her shoe, for a flipping start?

"And if you don't tell me very soon, I'm going to call the **police**!"

Gordon flipping Bennet, thought Norm. She was going to call the police if he didn't tell her his name? That was a bit harsh, wasn't it?

"Well?" said the woman, rapidly running out of what little patience she'd had to begin with.

"But ..." began Norm.

"Don't you but *me*, young man!" said the woman. "I'll give you one more chance to tell me who you are and, more importantly, what on earth you think you're doing trying to enter my house illegally?"

Uh? thought Norm. *Her* house? *Illegally?* Had the rest of the world gone stark raving mad? Or was it just him? If not, what the heck was going on? Because *he* hadn't got a flipping *clue* any more. Not that he'd had all that *much* of a clue in the first flipping place!

The woman tilted her head and eyed Norm quizzically. All of a sudden, she didn't seem *quite* so angry. In fact, she suddenly seemed quite concerned. Almost sympathetic.

"Are you *OK*?"

"Pardon?" said Norm.

"I said, are you feeling all right?"

Norm thought for a moment. **Was** he feeling all right? He'd been **perfectly** all right up until about thirty seconds ago. But now he wasn't so sure.

"Hello, Norman!" said a girl walking up the drive. "What are **you** doing here?"

Norm looked at the girl. She seemed **vaguely** familiar. He must have seen her **somewhere** before. But where?

"Norman?" said the woman. "So you **know** this boy?"

Either that, thought Norm, or it was an incredibly lucky guess.

"Yeah," said the girl. "We're in the same class for geography."

"We **are**?" said Norm, looking at her again. "I mean, we are, yeah."

The girl burst out laughing. "See, Mum? I **told** you he was funny, didn't I?"

"Oh, **that** Norman!" said the girl's mum. "You should have said, Ellie!"

Ellie? thought Norm. Nope. Still didn't ring any bells. And what did her mum mean, by '**that** Norman'? How many Normans did she flipping **know**? Because Norm didn't know **any**. Apart from himself. And he was pretty sure **that** didn't count. And anyway, how come they'd been talking about him? When **he** hadn't got a clue who **they** were? This wasn't just **weird**, thought Norm. This was actually a little bit **spooky**.

"Have you done the homework yet, by the way?" said Ellie.

"Homework?" said Norm. "What homework?"

"The **geography** homework, of course!" said Ellie.

Norm looked at Ellie as if she'd just stepped off a

12

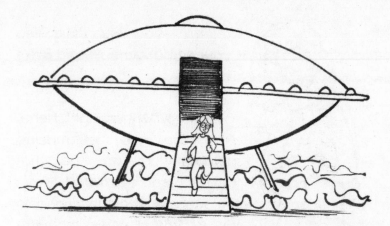

spaceship. Not only did he not have the faintest idea what she was on about, but he was beginning to wonder if this was all part of some elaborate practical joke and that he was actually being secretly filmed for some stupid TV show. It was an unlikely explanation, but right then it was the best Norm could come up with.

"I think your friend's a little discombobulated," said Ellie's mum.

A little **what**? thought Norm. Now she was just making random words up. And what did she mean, her **friend**? Norm was scarcely aware that Ellie had even **existed** till a few moments ago. And now all of a sudden they were flipping **friends**?

"'Scuse me a minute," said Norm, fishing his phone out of his pocket and opening up his maps app in order to try and find out where he was. Because by now it was fairly obvious that wherever it was, it wasn't where he thought he was.

"I didn't hear your phone go," said Ellie.

"What?" said Norm. "Er, no, I'm just . . ."

Ellie's mum smiled knowingly. "Lost?"

Norm nodded sheepishly.

"*Lost?*" said Ellie. "How can you be *lost*?"

"Aw, stop teasing him, Ellie."

Yeah, thought Norm. But it was too late. He could already feel himself going bright red.

"Well, he only lives around the *corner*," giggled Ellie.

He *did*? thought Norm, still looking at his phone. Oh, yeah. He *did*. And anyway, how come *she* knew where he lived? This wasn't just *spooky* any more. This was starting to get pretty flipping *creepy*.

"Don't worry about it, Norman," said Ellie's mum. "These things happen."

Norm sighed. These things happened, all right. In fact, these things happened a little too often as far as *he* was concerned. Not that Norm had actually ever got lost and mixed his house up with another house entirely before. But rubbish things in general happened a little too often. Well, if you were *Norm* they did, anyway. And Norm *was*.

CHAPTER 2

Ellie **and** Norm's map app were both right. Norm **did** live just around the corner. It wasn't like he'd been **miles** away, or the other side of town or anything. Not that he'd have been all that far away if he **had** been on the other side of town, what with it only being a fairly **small** town. It wasn't like it was a vast sprawling metropolis. Nowhere was **that** far from anywhere.

Norm just hadn't been concentrating, that was all. Well, he **had** been concentrating. Just not on what he was **supposed** to be concentrating on. He'd simply turned into the wrong street. It wasn't that big a deal. It wasn't even a medium-sized deal. These things happened, as Ellie's mum had said. And in fairness to Norm, Ellie's street **did** look an awful lot like his **own** street. Then again, one row of identical rabbit hutches was pretty much the same as any other as far as Norm was concerned. Not that they actually **were** rabbit hutches, of course.

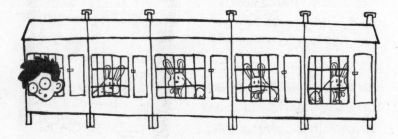

But compared to his old house they **seemed** rabbit hutches. Not that Norm's **old** house had been **especially** big. Far from it, in fact. His old house had been perfectly average. It's just that the **new** one was even **smaller** than average. Quite a **lot** smaller than average, actually. And Norm

still hadn't got used to it. And as far as Norm was concerned, he never flipping **would** get used to it. Even if he never moved again and ended up living in the same teensy little house until he was a hundred.

It turned out it didn't even **matter** that Norm was late. He hadn't been particularly missed. Or missed at all, actually. No one had even **noticed**. Partly because he was only a few minutes late. But mainly because everybody was too busy doing his – or in the case of Norm's mum, **her** – own thing. Which was perfectly fine by Norm, by the way. The **last** thing he wanted was to create a scene or give his parents the slightest excuse to kick off the second he walked through the flipping door.

Which seemed to happen all too often these days, if you asked Norm. Or even if you **didn't** ask him. But if no one batted an eyelid when he came in? Brilliant. Because all Norm was interested in was eating and then getting out on his bike as quickly as possible. And if he could manage to do that without being asked all the usual **boring** questions? That would be even **more** brilliant.

"What's for tea?" said Norm, walking into the kitchen and sitting down.

"Excuse me?" said Norm's dad, looking up from his laptop.

"What's for tea?" repeated Norm a bit louder, as if

his dad hadn't actually heard him.

"It would be nice to say hello first, love," said Norm's mum from next to the sink, where she was busy washing salad. Not that Norm knew that. Or cared.

"What?" said Norm. "Oh, right. Hello."

"Hello," said Norm's mum.

"What's for tea?" said Norm.

"*Excuse* me?" said Norm's dad, the vein on the side of his head immediately beginning to throb. A sure-fire sign that he was getting stressed. Not that Norm ever actually *noticed* his dad getting stressed. Then again, Norm's dad could get the words 'I'm getting stressed' tattooed across his forehead and Norm probably *still* wouldn't notice. But that wasn't the point. The point was that Norm had been home less than a minute and already his parents were kicking off, as usual. Well, his *dad* was, anyway.

"How was school?" asked Norm's mum, who actually **could** tell when Norm's dad was getting stressed and who was doing her best to change the subject as quickly as possible.

"What?" said Norm.

"**Pardon!**" said Norm's dad.

"Nothing. I just said **what**, that's all."

"Yes, I **know** you did!" said Norm's dad.

Gordon flipping **Bennet**, thought Norm. So if his dad had **known** what he'd said, why flipping **ask** then?

"I meant, say **pardon**, not **what**!"

Norm pulled a face. "What? I mean, **pardon**? I mean ..."

22

"So, how was it?" said Norm's mum.

"How was what?" said Norm.

"**School?**"

Norm sighed. Being asked about school was **precisely** the kind of stupid, boring question he'd hoped **not** to be asked. Because he never knew what to flipping say. Not that that ever stopped his parents from asking it. How **was** school? wondered Norm. It was a bit like the question itself. Completely pointless. Not that Norm would ever say **that**, of course. Or, at least not out loud he wouldn't, anyway.

SCHOOL = POINTLESS

"Well, love?" said Norm's mum. "How was it?"

"Oh, right," said Norm. "It was all right, I suppose."

"You **suppose**?"

Norm sighed again.

"Is there a problem, Norman?" said Norm's dad irritably. Not that Norm noticed **that**, either.

"How long have you got?" muttered Norm under his breath. But obviously slightly louder than he'd intended.

"What was that, Norman?" said his dad.

"Er, nothing," said Norm quickly.

"How long have I **got**?" said Norm's dad.

Norm pulled another face. His dad had done it again. What was the point of asking all these flipping **questions** if he already knew the flipping **answers**? But before the situation could escalate any further, Norm's two little brothers burst into the kitchen like a hurricane, followed by John the dog – a Cockapoo – who immediately sat down and started licking himself in the unmentionables. And for once, Norm was actually quite glad to see them. Not John's unmentionables. His brothers. Because at least it meant that he wasn't the focus of attention any longer. Not that Norm ever **was** the focus of attention for very long these days. Not since Brian was born he wasn't, anyway. And **definitely** not since Dave was born a couple of years after **that**. If, in fact, his brothers had actually been **born** in the first place and not created in some kind of laboratory by evil scientists. And, frankly, Norm still wasn't entirely convinced that they hadn't been.

"What's for tea?" said Brian, plonking himself down at the table.

"Pizza," said Norm's mum matter-of-factly, without even bothering to turn around.

"WHAAAAAAAT?" bellowed Norm, like a buffalo with bellyache. Not that Norm had ever actually seen or **heard** a buffalo with bellyache before, of course. But that wasn't the flipping point. The flipping **point** was how come **his brothers** could waltz in and ask what was for tea, but if **he** did that his parents went abso-flipping-lutely ballistic? It was **so** flipping unfair!

"Excuse me?" said Norm's dad.

"Why, Dad?" grinned Dave from the other side of the table. "What have you done?"

Brian laughed. "Good one, Dave!"

"Shut up, Brian, you little freak!" hissed Norm venomously.

"Language!" said Dave.

"And *you* can shut up as well, Dave!" said Norm.

"That's enough, Norman!" said Norm's dad.

"But ..."

"I said, that's *enough*!"

"Yeah, Norman," said Brian.

"Yeah, Norman," echoed Dave.

Gordon flipping **Bennet**, thought Norm. One of these flipping days he was going to literally explode with frustration. And **then** they'd be flipping sorry. Then again, thought Norm, knowing **his** flipping luck, if he actually **did** explode with frustration, he'd probably have to clear up the mess afterwards.

"What **kind** of pizza, Mum?" said Dave.

"Margherita," said Norm's mum.

"Mmmm, yum," said Dave. "My favourite."

Norm thought for a moment. Margherita pizza was **his** favourite too. Preferably twelve-inch deep-pan. And **preferably** accompanied by garlic bread and a portion of potato wedges with barbecue sauce. Definitely no salad, which in Norm's opinion was only fit for consumption by **rabbits**.

"Takeaway?" asked Brian hopefully.

"Ooh, yeah!" said Dave. "Wikipizza?"

"'Fraid not," laughed Norm's mum.

"Aw!" chorused Brian and Dave together.

"Not today, boys," said Norm's dad.

Of **course** not, thought Norm bitterly. Because that would have been a bit **too** much to ask, wouldn't it? What had he and his brothers ever done to deserve such luxury? And besides, why bother splashing out on the finest home-delivered pizza known to mankind when you could buy flipping supermarket own-brand pizza instead, for a fraction of the flipping price?

"When, then?" said Norm.

Everything suddenly went very quiet. Even John stopped doing what he was doing and looked up.

"What did you say, Norman?" said Norm's dad.

Norm had a pretty good idea that this was yet another instance of his dad knowing perfectly **well** what he'd just said. He also had a pretty good idea that his dad **knew** that Norm knew that he knew perfectly well what he'd just said, but that Norm was expected to repeat it anyway, for dramatic purposes.

"I was just wondering **when** we might next have a Wikipizza, Dad," said Norm. "That's all."

Norm's dad paused. And when Norm's dad paused, it was as if the earth stopped revolving and time stood still.

"That's **all**?" he said eventually.

Norm shrugged. Which merely had the effect of making Norm's dad seem even **more** stressed than he was already – and the vein on the side of his head throb even faster. Not that Norm noticed.

"How **old** are you, Norman?" said Norm's dad quietly.

Not suitable for under 13s

How old was he? thought Norm. What had *that* got to do with anything? His dad might as well ask him to name ten types of fish, or what the flipping capital of Belgium was! Unless age restrictions on eating pizzas had suddenly been introduced without Norm's knowledge? And, frankly, if they had and Norm wasn't legally allowed to eat pizza in this country any more, he was going to emigrate to somewhere where he flipping well *was*. And anyway, thought Norm, how come his own dad didn't know how old he was? He knew his parents had been a bit preoccupied with other stuff lately, but this was ridiculous!

"Answer your dad, love," said Norm's mum, stepping in again and acting as the peacemaker. Or at least trying to.

"What?" said Norm. "I mean, pardon?"

"Dad asked how old you were," said Dave.

Brian looked puzzled. "Were, or **are**?"

Norm sighed wearily. "I'm nearly thirteen."

"So, twelve then," said Brian.

"What?" said Norm irritably.

"Technically, you're still twelve," said Brian.

"Yeah, whatever, Brian," said Norm. "And **technically** you're still an idiot."

"Muuuum! Daaaaad!" wailed Brian. "Norman just called me an idiot!"

"They're still here, you know," said Dave.

"What?" said Brian.

"Mum and Dad," said Dave. "They're still here. So they *know* Norman just called you an idiot."

"Yeah, I know but ..." began Brian.

"Idiot," muttered Norm, who was still wondering what the connection between his age and Margherita pizzas was. If indeed there actually *was* a connection.

"I remember when *I* was twelve," said Norm's dad.

"Nearly thirteen," said Norm.

"Norman!" said Norm's mum, shooting him a look.

"You were twelve once, Dad?" said Dave.

"What do *you* think, Dave?" said Brian. "Of *course* Dad was twelve once!"

"Whoah!" said Dave, as if the thought of his dad being anything but the age he was *now* was completely unimaginable, let alone the thought that he was once the same age as *Norm*.

"I remember *I* thought money grew on trees too," said Norm's dad. "That there were endless reserves of the stuff. That whatever I wanted I could get just by clicking my fingers. That I was somehow ***entitled*** to it. That ***my*** mum and dad had bottomless pockets."

"Better than bottomless ***trousers***," whispered Dave.

"What?" whispered Brian.

"Sssshhhh, you two!" said Norm's mum.

"Norman?" said Norm's dad.

But Norm didn't reply. His eyes were closed. Or at least they **were** until Dave gave him a sharp dig in the ribs with his elbow.

"Ow! Uh? What? Who?" said Norm groggily.

"Were you *asleep*?" said Norm's dad.

"What?" said Norm. "No, I was just ..."

"Just what?"

Norm thought for a moment. "Just taking a long time to blink."

Brian and Dave both tried, not very successfully, to stifle sniggers.

"Are you trying to be funny, Norman?" said Norm's dad. "Because if you are—"

There was a sudden knock on the front door. Whatever it was that Norm's dad was going to do if Norm was trying to be funny would just have to wait. And, once again, Norm **was** very grateful for a distraction.

"I'll get it," he said, standing up and heading for the hall.

CHAPTER 3

Norm was surprised to find Mikey standing outside when he opened the front door. After all, they'd

only just seen each other at school a short time earlier. And, as far as Norm knew, they hadn't made any arrangements to meet *after* school. Not that you actually *needed* to make arrangements to see your best friend, of course. Or any friend for that matter. But if you were best friends – and had been since you were running around together in nappies, or rather, **crawling** around together in nappies, at parent and toddler group, you could turn up pretty much whenever you wanted. Within **reason**, of course. Visits in the middle of the night weren't generally encouraged. But apart from that, it was considered acceptable to appear anytime you liked. And **without** having made an appointment first.

"All right?" said Norm.

"All right?" said Mikey.

They looked at each other for a moment.

"So?" said Norm.

"So, what?" said Mikey.

"Uh?" said Norm. "What do you mean, so what? You came round **here**, Mikey! No one **made** you."

"Yeah, I know," said Mikey.

"So you can't just stand there like a flipping doughnut."

"Yeah, I know," said Mikey again.

They looked at each other for another, slightly longer moment.

"Well?" said Norm, getting more and more exasperated.

"Well, **what**?" said Mikey.

"Gordon flipping **Bennet**, Mikey!" said Norm, who was beginning to wish someone **else** had answered the door instead. Because if he stood there much longer he was going to have to start **shaving**.

"Aren't you going to ask me in or something?" said Mikey.

"No," said Norm.

"Why not?" said Mikey.

Norm shrugged his shoulders. "Not much point if you're not going to **say** anything, is there? And anyway, we haven't had our tea yet."

"That's OK," said Mikey. "I won't be long. I just need to have a quick word with your mum and dad."

"WHAAAT?"

said Norm, as if Mikey had just announced that he

was thinking of resigning from the human race and becoming a penguin instead.

"That's why I've come round," said Mikey.

"But ..."

"What?" said Mikey.

Norm pulled a face. Frankly, if *he* had a choice, *he* wouldn't *ever* talk to his mum and dad. So why on earth would *Mikey* want to? That wasn't just *strange*. That was unbe-flipping-lievable.

"Are they in?" said Mikey.

"Who?"

"Your mum and dad," said Mikey. "Obviously."

"Seriously, Mikey?" said Norm. "You really want to *talk* to my mum and dad?"

Mikey nodded. "Yeah."

"Actually *talk* to them?"

"Yeah, why not?" said Mikey. "What's wrong with that?"

"What's *wrong* with it?" said Norm. "They're my mum and dad! *That's* what's flipping *wrong* with it, Mikey!"

Mikey looked puzzled. "There's nothing wrong with your mum and dad."

"**_Seriously?_**" said Norm. "Are you winding me up?"

"WHO IS IT, LOVE?" called Norm's mum from the kitchen.

"ONLY ME!" called Mikey.

"MIKEY?"

"HI THERE!" yelled Mikey.

"YEAH! BIKEY MIKEY!" yelled Brian and Dave together.

"AREN'T YOU GOING TO ASK HIM IN, NORMAN?" called Norm's dad.

"Gordon flipping Bennet," grumbled Norm, reluctantly standing to one side and letting Mikey casually saunter past as if *he* lived there and not the other way around. If it wasn't *already* one of those flipping days, it flipping was *now*.

CHAPTER 4

By the time Norm had closed the door again and followed Mikey into the kitchen, Mikey had already sat down at the table. In **his** place.

"Oi," said Norm. "That's my seat."

"Correction," said Norm's dad. "It **was** your seat, Norman. Mikey's sitting there now."

Norm sighed. He could flipping **see** that. And he wasn't very happy about it, either.

"Yeah, Norman," said Brian.

"Yeah, Norman," said Dave.

"And anyway," said Brian, "it's not *your* seat."

"What?" said Norm.

"It doesn't actually **belong** to you. Technically it belongs to Mum and Dad."

Norm glared at his middle brother like an eagle eyeing up a rabbit. Was it his imagination, or was Brian being even *more* annoying than usual? And *that* was flipping saying something.

"And to what do we owe the pleasure, Mikey?" said Norm's mum, who by now had finished at the sink and was also sitting down at the table, on the one remaining seat.

"Pardon?" said Mikey.

Yeah, thought Norm. What on earth did *that* flipping mean? Why was his mum talking all posh like that? It was only **Mikey**. Not some member of the royal family.

"What brings you here?" said Norm's mum. "Did you want something in particular?"

"Oh, right, I see," said Mikey. "Er, yeah. My mum and dad were just wondering what you're doing tomorrow night?"

Norm looked at his best friend for a second. Had he **really** just said what Norm **thought** he'd just said? That **Mikey's** mum and dad wanted to know what **his** mum and dad were doing tomorrow night? Because if so, that could only mean one thing. Well, actually, thought Norm, it could mean a couple of things. Firstly it could mean that Mikey's mum and dad were just incredibly nosy and liked to know everything that everybody else was up to. And that was all. End of. But much more worryingly it could **also** mean – and almost certainly **did** mean – that Mikey's mum and dad were going to ask **Norm's** mum and dad to do something.

Together. Otherwise it would be a bit stupid and pointless asking. And the mere **thought** of his parents at any kind of public gathering was enough to make Norm's toes curl with embarrassment.

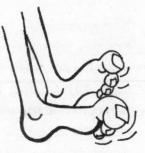

"You mean, just Norman's dad and I?" said Norm's mum.

Mikey nodded.

Gordon flipping Bennet, thought Norm, as his mum and dad looked at each other. It was like something out of a scary movie. You knew something bad was about to happen. You just didn't know **what**.

"Nothing, I don't think, are we?" said Norm's mum.

"Don't think so, no," said Norm's dad.

"You're not thinking of taking me out for a surprise romantic dinner somewhere, then?"

"Ha ha, no," laughed Norm's dad.

Thank goodness, thought Norm. Because **that** would have been scarier than **any** flipping **movie** he could **ever** think of. And anyway, how come his dad had changed his tune all of a sudden? A few minutes ago he was all set to blow his flipping top. Now here he was being all nice and friendly, as if nothing had ever **happened**. Then again, thought Norm, if his

dad really **was** thinking of taking his mum out for a surprise dinner, he was hardly going to **say** that he was. Otherwise it wouldn't be much of a flipping surprise any more, would it?

"Why do you ask, Mikey?" said Norm's mum.

Yeah, thought Norm. Why **had** Mikey asked? Because if Mikey's mum and dad really **were** going to ask **his** mum and dad to do something together tomorrow night, then he really needed to know what it was as soon as possible so that he could at least **begin** to get his head around the idea and prepare himself for the inevitable horrors to come. Not that it was likely to be anything **too** horrific or embarrassing, knowing **Mikey's** mum and dad. They were usually pretty cool. Well, for adults they were, anyway. They were certainly a lot cooler than his **own** parents.

Then again, thought Norm, just about **anybody**'s parents were cooler than his **own** parents. But **Mikey's** parents were actually all right. They always seemed really chilled and laid back. At least, they were whenever Norm saw them. He'd never even heard them raise their voices at Mikey, let alone seen them have a row about anything. To be honest, he couldn't imagine what they'd ever actually have a row **about**. Because money didn't seem to be an issue as far as Norm could see. Or rather, **lack** of money didn't seem to be an issue as far as Norm could see. He'd certainly never noticed anything own-brand in **Mikey's** house! **And** Mikey's mum made **the** best hot chocolate in the entire flipping universe. Never mind a win-win situation. It was more like a win-win situation with whipped cream and a flipping **flake** sticking out at the top.

"Mikey?" said Norm's mum.

"What? Oh, yeah, sorry," said Mikey, fishing in his back pocket before pulling out a folded leaflet and handing it to Norm's mum.

"What's this?" she said, unfolding it.

Just flipping **read** it and find **out**, thought Norm, barely able to contain his frustration. Because if **he** didn't find out soon he was going to go off like a flipping **rocket**.

"**Salsa** Night?" said Norm's mum.

"Sounds intriguing," said Norm's dad.

Sounds flipping **weird**, more like, thought Norm. A whole evening devoted to a kind of spicy sauce that you dip your Doritos into? Is that really what people did when they got old?

Because if so, he was perfectly happy to stay the same age for ever.

"There's just one teensy problem," said Norm's mum.

Just **one**? thought Norm. Because he could think of **several** problems. And none of them were particularly 'teensy'. For a start, they only had **one** toilet between them ever since they'd moved to this stupid little house. And after a night of doing nothing except consuming **salsa**, his mum and dad could well be needing one **each** the following morning.

"Yeah," said Norm's dad. "We don't know how to do it."

"Do **what**?" said Brian.

"Dance," said Norm's mum. "Well, not **that** kind of dance, anyway."

Norm was getting very confused. What had salsa got to do with dancing? Unless, of course, the whole idea was that you ate your Doritos **whilst** dancing? But surely that would be quite tricky, wouldn't it? Not to mention extremely messy and potentially dangerous too.

"My parents will show you how," said Mikey.

"Your mum and dad know how to salsa?" said Norm's mum, clearly impressed.

Uh? thought Norm. **How** to salsa? Or how to **make** salsa?

"Oh, they're not **experts** or anything," said Mikey. "But they're OK, I suppose. They do it around the house, anyway. It's quite embarrassing, actually."

Norm pulled a face. Did **what** around the house? What was everybody **talking** about? He could see their mouths moving but the sounds they were making made no sense whatso-flipping-**ever**. It was like he was watching a foreign movie without **realising** it. Actually, thought Norm, that was **exactly** what it was like. Much more of this and he was going to have to change channels.

"Anyway, it doesn't matter," said Mikey. "It's all for charity."

Norm sighed. What difference did it make if it was for flipping *charity* or not? What had ***that*** got to do with anything? And what so-called *charity* was this so-called 'Salsa Night' in aid of, anyway? Because if ***anyone*** deserved charity it was ***him***. Not many people had to put up with what ***he*** had to put up with. Two skinflint parents? A smelly dog? Even smellier brothers? A house the size of a flipping shoe box? Supermarket own-brand ***pizza***? Never mind *charity*, thought Norm. ***He*** deserved a flipping ***medal***!

"What charity's that, then, Mikey?" said Norm's dad.

"SOS?" said Dave.

"What's that stand for?" said Brian.

"Save Our Squirrels," said Dave.

"Really?" said Brian.

"Nah, not really. I just made it up," said Dave. "Good though, isn't it?"

"Not bad, actually," said Brian.

Gordon flipping **Bennet**, muttered Norm to himself.

"Oh, wait a minute, it says here," said his mum, looking more closely at the leaflet and reading. "Help raise funds to build schools in Africa."

What? thought Norm. Actually **build** schools? What would you want to do **that** for?

SALSA NIGHT

Help raise funds to build schools in Africa

If there was a charity that raised money to knock schools **down**, that would be different. In fact, if there was a charity that raised money to knock schools **down**, thought Norm, he'd be the first to volunteer to drive the flipping **bulldozer**! But actually **build** schools? Surely there were enough

of those by now, weren't there? No, what the world **really** needed was more places to go mountain biking. Well, more places for **Norm** to go mountain biking, anyway. There were no mountains anywhere **near** where he lived. Which wasn't flipping fair, for a start. So if anyone wanted to raise money and build one of **those** – and preferably in Norm's back garden – they'd be **more** than welcome.

"How much?" said Norm's dad.

"For the tickets?" said Mikey.

Norm's dad nodded.

"Ten pounds," said Mikey.

"Ten pounds?" said Norm, his eyes widening in amazement.

"Each," said Mikey.

"Ten pounds *each*?" squawked Norm like an incredulous parrot. "That's ..."

"Twenty pounds altogether," interjected Brian.

"Good boy, Brian," said Norm's mum.

Good boy? thought Norm. For knowing that ten plus flipping ten equalled flipping twenty? But actually, thinking about it, thought Norm thinking about it, he really ought to be quite *grateful* to Brian. Because at least it had stopped Norm from saying what he *wanted* to say. And what he was *about* to say. Which was that in *his* opinion, twenty pounds for going to some stupid dance, or whatever it flipping was, was nothing short of **scandalous**. Especially when you considered that that twenty pounds could be put to **far** better use than building flipping schools in Africa. Like buying a twelve-inch deep-pan Margherita pizza from Wikipizza for a flipping start. With garlic bread and a portion of potato wedges. And **barbecue** sauce. Not flipping **salsa** sauce. Then again, thought Norm, some things were best left unsaid. And that was probably one of them.

"Can **we** go?" said Brian.

"Ooh, yeah," said Dave. "Can we? Can we? Can we?"

"Pleeeeeeeeeeeeeeeease?" sang Brian and Dave together.

"I'm afraid not, boys," said Norm's mum.

"Awwwwwwwwwwwwwwww!" wailed Brian and Dave.

"No, I'm sorry," said Norm's mum, reading from the leaflet again, "but it says here that you have to be at least twelve to go."

"Aw, 'snot fair!" huffed Dave.

Welcome to my flipping **world**, thought Norm.

Norm's mum turned to Norm. "You can come if you like though, love?"

Norm looked at his mum as if she'd just suggested that he went to school wearing nothing except his pants. "Seriously?"

"Sure. Why not?" said Norm's mum.

Why **not**? thought Norm.

Because his mum and dad would have to pay **him** twenty pounds every day for the rest of his life before he'd even **consider** going to something as skull-crushingly boring and trouser-wettingly embarrassing as a so-called flipping **Salsa Night**! And even then he'd **still** say no. **That** was why not!

"Is that a yes, then?" said Norm's mum.

"What?" said Norm. "No, it's **not**!"

"So it's a no, then?"

"No," said Norm. "I mean, yes it's a no. I mean ..."

"Hey. I've got an idea," said Brian. "What if Dave sits on my shoulders and we wear a really long coat and **pretend** to be Norm?"

"Yeah!" said Dave. "Can we? Can we? Can we?"

"Pleeeeeeeeeeeeease?" wailed Brian.

"I can irritate him," said Dave.

"Pardon?" said Norm's dad.

"I can **irritate** Norman," said Dave.

Flipping **right** he could, thought Norm. But this wasn't exactly earth-shattering news. Dave had been irritating him for **years**, same as Brian had. Still, it was nice of him to finally **admit** it.

Norm's mum laughed. "You mean, **imitate** him?"

"What?" said Dave. "Yeah. That's what I meant. I can **imitate** him."

"Go on, then," urged Brian. "Show them, Dave."

Everyone turned to look at Dave expectantly. Even Norm.

"Shut up, Dave, you little freak!" said Dave, doing his best to make his voice as deep and grumpy and generally as Norm-like as possible. But still basically sounding like Dave.

"What?" said Norm. "I don't sound anything *like* that, you *doughnut*."

Norm's mum laughed again. "You do a *bit*, love."

Norm sighed. "Seriously?"

"It was quite good actually, Norm," said Mikey.

Gordon flipping *Bennet*, thought Norm. So other people could say what he sounded like, but he *couldn't*? Next thing he knew they'd be telling him what he was flipping *thinking*!

"Anyway, you still can't go, boys, and that's all there is to it," said Norm's dad. "Rules are rules."

"Stupid rules," mumbled Brian.

"So flipping unfair," said Dave, still imitating Norm. Or at least trying to, anyway.

"On the *plus* side," said Norm's dad with a grin, "Grandpa can baby-sit for you!"

"Really?" said Brian, brightening immediately.

"Of course."

"YEAAAAAAAAAAAAAAAAH!!!" yelled Brian and Dave, suddenly all smiles again.

"If he's free, boys," said Norm's mum.

Norm thought for a moment. So his mum and dad would only ask Grandpa to baby-sit if he was *free*? Gordon flipping **Bennet**. He knew they were tight-fisted, but he didn't know they were *that* tight-fisted. Surely they could afford to pay Grandpa a *couple* of quid, couldn't they?

There was a sudden burst of classical music from Mikey's trousers.

"Sorry, I'd better get this," he said, producing his phone from a pocket and answering it. "Oh, hi, Dad." Mikey smiled apologetically and put his free hand over the phone's mouthpiece. "It's my dad."

No, really? thought Norm. He would never have known.

"Yeah, I've given it to them," said Mikey on the phone again. "They seem quite keen."

Norm's mum nodded and smiled at Mikey.

"What? You mean now?" said Mikey. "'Kay, Dad. I'll be back in a few minutes. Yeah, bye."

Everyone watched as Mikey ended the call and put his phone back in his pocket.

"Sounds like you've got to go, Mikey," said Norm's dad.

Mikey nodded. "Yeah. 'Fraid so."

"But ..." began Norm.

"What?" said Mikey.

"What about biking?"

"What about it?" said Norm's dad.

"Erm, well, I was hoping to go, Dad," said Norm.

"Oh, you were, were you?"

"Perhaps you'd like to run that by us first, love?" added Norm's mum.

Uh? thought Norm. Why would he want to do *that*? What had going *biking* got to do with his mum and dad? Unless *they* wanted to come as well? And, quite honestly, there was more chance of them winning the flipping lottery than there was of *that* ever happening. And, as far as Norm knew, his mum and dad didn't even *do* the lottery.

"Well?" said his dad.

Norm pulled a face. This was all making about as

much sense as a two-sided triangle.

"Anyway, I can't," said Mikey.

"Can't what?" said Norm.

Mikey looked at Norm for a moment. "Go biking."

Norm laughed. "Good one, Mikey."

"What do you mean?" said Mikey.

"Very funny."

"I'm not joking, Norm," said Mikey.

"But we **always** go biking after school on Fridays!" said Norm.

"I know," said Mikey. "But I can't **today**. That's why my dad called. I've got to go home and practise—"

Mikey stopped mid-sentence, as if someone had suddenly switched him off at the mains. He'd clearly been about to say something else, but for some reason he'd decided **not** to.

"You've got to go home and practise **what**?" said Norm.

Mikey looked at Norm for a moment. "Nothing. Gotta go, Norm. Bye."

"What do you mean, **nothing**?" said Norm. "You just said ..."

But it was too late. Mikey had already gone.

CHAPTER 5

Having demolished the supermarket own-brand Margherita pizza and **no** salad in record time, Norm headed straight outside and opened the garage door. It was early Friday evening. It was still light. There wasn't a cloud in sight. Not that Norm would have noticed if there **had** been a cloud in sight. Frankly, Norm wouldn't have noticed if his house was about to be hit by a tornado the size of Belgium. But for the time being at least, all was well in Norm's world. Well, all was **relatively** well in Norm's world, anyway. Norm couldn't actually remember the last time

all had been 100 per cent well in his world. Frankly, he wasn't entirely sure that all had *ever* been 100 per cent well in his world. But things were *reasonably* OK. Which, admittedly, was better than being completely rubbish. And just because *Mikey* couldn't go biking, didn't mean that *he* couldn't.

There was just one little thing still gnawing away at the back of Norm's mind, like a dog chewing on a bone. Actually, not such a little thing at all, thought Norm. Quite a big thing, really. Actually an *enormous* thing. Like a really *massive* dog chewing on a really *massive* bone. Why on earth had Mikey

Hallå!

suddenly had to go home? What was it that he had to practise all of a sudden? His twelve times tables? The tuba? Swedish? No, thought Norm. Because none of those things were even remotely as important as *biking*. Then again, thought Norm, *nothing* was more important than *biking*. And nothing ever *would* be.

Norm had been into bikes and biking all his life. Well, ever since he'd been old enough to actually *ride* one, he had. And not *all* his life, obviously. Not yet, anyway. But he'd certainly been into bikes and biking for *most* of his life so *far*. While other kids dreamt of being footballers and pop stars, all *Norm* had ever dreamt of was zooming down hillsides and of one day fulfilling his **_ultimate_** dream. Standing on top of the winner's podium at the World Mountain Biking Championships, holding the trophy in the air.

For now though, Norm was just going to have to make do with a quick ride through the woods and maybe jumping the steps at the shopping precinct before it got too dark. It definitely wasn't a good idea to ride through the woods **_after_** it got dark. In an argument between a bike and a tree there was only ever one winner. And it **_wasn't_** the bike, as Norm had found out to his cost on more than one occasion.

Well, not **his** cost. But his mum and dad's cost. Back in the days when they used to have money and could actually afford to **pay** for the repairs. Anyway, Norm needed to get a bit of a shift on if he wanted a half-decent ride. Because his lights weren't working and, despite his mum's best efforts to convince him to eat carrots because they helped him see in the dark, Norm still **couldn't** see in the dark. And anyway, he hated flipping carrots.

"Hello, **Norman**!" said an all-too-familiar voice as Norm emerged from the gloom of the garage, wearing his helmet and wheeling his bike beside him.

Gordon flipping **Bennet**, thought Norm, looking round to see Chelsea peering over the fence. Not that he actually **needed** to turn around to see who it was. He **knew** who it was the second she'd opened her mouth and over-emphasised his name as if it was the funniest thing she'd ever heard. Just like she'd done a **billion** times before. And no doubt just like she would a **billion** times again in future. And even if she **hadn't** said anything, there was only ever **one** person who had a habit of popping up like a flipping jack-in-the-box the split second Norm appeared on the drive.

And that was **Chelsea**. His next-door neighbour.

"What's up?"

"Nothing," said Norm.

"Nothing?" said Chelsea. "Could've fooled me."

Norm sighed. It really was quite incredible just how quickly Chelsea could wind him up. She could do it even quicker than his little brothers could. And

that was no mean feat, because Brian and Dave didn't even have to be in the same **room** as Norm to wind him up, sometimes. They just had to **exist**. But Chelsea? She seemed to take the art of winding up to a whole new level. If it was a **martial** art she'd **definitely** be black belt. In fact, if it was a **martial** art, Chelsea would be an **instructor**. Others would come to her to **learn**.

"So?" said Chelsea.

"So what?" said Norm.

"Why aren't you talking to me, then?"

Norm thought for a moment. Why wasn't he **talking** to Chelsea? How long had she flipping **got**? Longer than **he'd** got, **that** was for sure.

"Well?" said Chelsea. "I'm waiting."

Norm was waiting, too. But in **his** case, he was waiting for Chelsea to disappear again and leave him in flipping peace.

Chelsea tilted her head to one side and looked at Norm. "Seriously, what's up, **Norman**? You look like someone just nicked your porridge!"

"I dunno what you're on about," said Norm.

"Really?" said Chelsea.

"Yeah, really," said Norm. "I don't even *like* porridge."

Chelsea smiled. "You know something?"

Norm sighed again. He knew *lots* of things. For instance, he knew that if Chelsea didn't shut up soon, it would be the middle of the flipping night before he got to go biking.

"You're funny," said Chelsea.

Norm looked at Chelsea. Even if he *could* be bothered to say something, he didn't know *what* to say. Because if he wasn't mistaken, that was a *compliment*, wasn't it? Or at least Norm *thought* it was. Then again, you never could tell with Chelsea. It might have *appeared* to be a compliment, but actually *wasn't*.

"Women find that very attractive, you know," said Chelsea.

Flutter Flutter

Uh, what? thought Norm. Had he missed something? Had someone accidentally pressed fast forward? Or had he actually dozed off for a second? Because he hadn't got a clue what Chelsea was on about any more. Not that he had all that much of an idea in the first flipping place.

"You knew that, didn't you, **Norman**?"

"Knew what?" said Norm.

"That women like men with a sense of humour?"

Instantly, alarm bells began ringing in Norm's head, so loudly that he looked around to see if anyone else could hear them. What exactly was Chelsea **saying**? That she found *him* attractive? And if so, why had she chosen *this* particular moment to say it, when she could have said it *before*? Because surely you didn't just suddenly fancy someone, did you? It wasn't like flicking a switch, or pressing a button. And anyway, thought Norm, he was nowhere near being a man yet. He was nearly *thirteen*, not nearly flipping *thirty*! There'd be plenty of time for all that gross kind of stuff in years to come, along with flipping Salsa Nights and trips to IKEA.

Once again, Norm had no idea how to respond. Or even, how he was *expected* to respond. The good ship Norm was entering uncharted waters. And things were beginning to look distinctly choppy.

"You look worried," said Chelsea.

Worried? thought Norm. He wasn't **worried**. He was abso-flipping-lutely **terrified**!

"**I** don't fancy **you**!" Chelsea said.

Norm looked at Chelsea. Had she just said what he **thought** she'd just said? Or was that just wishful thinking?

"Sorry, what?"

"I said **I** don't fancy **you**," said Chelsea.

OK, thought Norm. So Chelsea **had** just said what he thought she'd said. But what now? Because Norm hadn't felt **this** relieved since he finally went to the toilet after being constipated for an entire week.

He wanted to jump for joy. He wanted to scream. He wanted to shout it from the rooftops. But he couldn't do that. Because that wouldn't be cool.

"Obviously," he said, as nonchalantly as possible.

"Yeah," said Chelsea, nodding. "Obviously. I wouldn't fancy **you** if you were the last person on earth, **Norman**."

Norm wasn't sure he knew how he felt about this. Because on the one hand he was genuinely **ecstatic** that he'd momentarily got hold of the wrong end of the stick, and that Chelsea **didn't** find him attractive, after all. It had only been for a few seconds but those few seconds were, without doubt, some of the worst seconds of Norm's life. And that **included** the time he'd woken up to find the dog sitting on his face, just after he'd farted. After the dog had farted. Not Norm. But on the other hand, Norm did actually feel just ever so slightly insulted. Did Chelsea **really** have to say **that**? That she wouldn't fancy him if he was the last person on earth? She could have just said that she didn't fancy him and left it there. But, **oh no**. She had to make a flipping point of just how **much** she didn't fancy him, didn't she? Talk about rubbing salt in the wound, or whatever that expression was, thought Norm. She might as well have said that she'd sooner snog the back of a flipping **bus** than **him**.

"No offence, **Norman**."

"What?" said Norm.

"No offence," said Chelsea. "That I don't fancy you."

Norm shrugged. "None taken."

"I'm sure someone will, though," said Chelsea. "Eventually."

Again, thought Norm, did she really have to add **that**? That someone would fancy him **eventually**? Was that actually supposed to make him feel **better**? Not that Norm was remotely bothered whether anyone was ever going to fancy him or not. Right now it was the **last** thing on his mind. And the **first** thing was, was Chelsea **ever** going to stop talking? Because at this flipping rate it was going to be the middle of the **next** flipping night before he set off biking!

"Oh, well," said Chelsea. "I'd better get on, I suppose."

"Yeah," mumbled Norm. "You better had."

Chelsea pulled a face. "What was that, **_Norman_**?"

"What?" said Norm. "Oh, nothing. I just said **_I'd_** better get on too."

"Hmmm," said Chelsea, eyeing Norm suspiciously, as if she didn't quite believe that's what he'd **really** said.

"What?" said Norm defensively. "I flipping well **_did_**!"

"Whatever," said Chelsea.

Norm gritted his teeth. He **hated** it when someone said **whatever** to **him**. It was OK when it was the other way round and **he** said it to someone **else**. But when **he** was the on the receiving end of a *whatever*? That wasn't on at all. And *especially* when he was on the receiving end of a *whatever* from *Chelsea*! That *really* wasn't on at all.

There was only one thing for it, thought Norm. He was going to have to say something so witheringly and bitingly sarcastic that Chelsea would think twice before ever *whatevering* him again. That would flipping show *her*! If only he could actually *think* of something. It was *so* flipping annoying.

"What's the matter, *Norman*?" said Chelsea. "You look like you've lost your llama."

"Whatever," said Norm, finally getting on his bike and pedalling off down the street.

"MISSING YOU ALREADY, **NORMAN**!" yelled Chelsea.

Gordon flipping **Bennet**, thought Norm, wobbling and almost falling off again.

CHAPTER 6

It was still light by the time Norm got to the shopping precinct. But not nearly as light as it **had** been when he'd got his bike out of the garage twenty minutes earlier. And certainly not as light as it **would** be if he didn't hurry up and start perfecting a few tricks and stunts and manoeuvres pretty flipping soon. Well, maybe not actually **perfecting** them, thought Norm, but definitely **working** on them and generally trying to **improve** them. How else was he ever going to get better? How else was he ever going to become World Mountain Biking Champion?

Norm thought for a moment as he wheelied, first past the newsagent and then the chemist. If there was *one* good thing about Mikey not being able to go biking with him – and there *was* only *one* thing that he could think of off the top of his head – it was that Norm wouldn't be constantly *comparing* himself to Mikey. Or rather, Norm wouldn't be constantly comparing his *biking* skills to *Mikey's*. Because there were *many* things that irritated Norm. His two brothers and Chelsea being three of them. But towards the very top of the list was the fact that Mikey was just that little bit better than Norm at *biking*.

Not that Norm actually *had* a list of all the things that irritated him. But if he did? Well, firstly it would

NORM'S MOST
irritating things
Chelsea
Mikey being
naturally brilliant
on two wheels
Brian
Dave

be a very long list. And secondly, his best friend being naturally brilliant on two wheels would be **right** up there. Norm could just about cope with Mikey being just that little bit better than him at **most** things. But Mikey being better at **biking** was what **really** irked him. Because it was **Norm** who was crazy about biking, not **Mikey**. It was **Norm** who thought about biking from the moment he got up to the moment he went to bed again, not **Mikey**. And it was **Norm** who dreamt about biking when he was actually **in** bed, not **Mikey**. It was not only oh-so-flipping **unfair**, thought Norm, but also oh-so-flipping **typical** of his so-called flipping **luck**.

Looking back on what happened next, it was hard for Norm to say at what point everything started going in slow motion. Whether it was the moment he first became aware of a furry blur, dashing out of a doorway and heading straight across his intended path, or whether it was the moment he slammed his brakes on and swerved in an effort to actually avoid **hitting** the furry blur. Either way, Norm somehow instinctively knew that if he **didn't** swerve and brake, it would be very bad news. Not only for **himself**, but for the furry blur, as well. Whatever the furry blur actually was. And at that precise moment in time, Norm didn't particularly **care** what it was either.

"GORDON FLIPPING BEN—" Norm began to yell. But even though everything had already started going in slow motion as far as *he* was concerned, like an explosion in an action movie, it all still happened **very** quickly. Before he knew what was happening, Norm – or strictly speaking, Norm's **bike** – was skidding uncontrollably and hurtling straight towards a concrete rubbish bin.

And a concrete rubbish bin, rather like a tree, was another one of those things you definitely didn't want to get into an argument with. At least, not when you were riding a bike it wasn't, anyway.

Not that Norm had time to actually **think** that. All **Norm** knew was that he only had a split second to jump if he didn't want to end up in hospital. And in **hospital** there'd be even **less** flipping chance of getting a twelve-inch deep-pan Margherita from Wikipizza than there was at home!

"Norman?" said a voice a moment later. Although, frankly, Norm couldn't have said whether it was a **moment** later, or three weeks later.

"Uh? What?" said Norm, looking up groggily to see Ellie peering anxiously at him. Not that Norm had actually **twigged** that it was Ellie yet. He scarcely knew what **planet** he was on, let alone who was **talking** to him.

"Are you OK?"

"Er, yeah, I **think** so," said Norm, getting up off the ground and dusting himself down. "Who are you, anyway?"

"Who **am** I?" said Ellie. "I'm Ellie!"

"Oh, right, yeah," said Norm, everything slowly beginning to swim back into focus.

"That was **incredible**."

Norm pulled a face. "What was?"

Ellie looked at Norm. "Are you **sure** you're OK?"

"Erm ..."

"Did you bump your head?"

"What?" said Norm.

"Come here!" said Ellie sternly.

"Uh?" said Norm.

"Not you, Norman," said Ellie. "I'm talking to Santa."

Santa? thought Norm. Maybe he **had** taken a bump to the head after all. If not, what was *Santa* doing in the flipping **precinct**? It was nowhere **near** Christmas. And even if it was, where would he park his sleigh?

"Santa!" yelled Ellie. "Stop that!"

Norm turned around just in time to see a dog cocking its leg and peeing on his bike.

"Bad dog!" said Ellie.

Gordon flipping **Bennet**, thought Norm. That was **all** he needed. And what was his bike doing over there, anyway? And how come **he** wasn't **on** it?

"Sorry," said Ellie. "And thanks, by the way."

"For what?" said Norm.

"For not hitting Santa."

"What?" said Norm. "So ..."

Ellie nodded. "He shot out in
front of you. And you swerved
out of the way and then jumped
off your bike like a stunt man. It
was amazing, actually! I wish
I'd been filming it with my
phone. But then, thinking
about it, why **would**
I have been filming it?
I'm not psychic."

"Right," said Norm.

"Can you not
remember?" said Ellie.

"Remember what?" said Norm.

"What I just **told** you!"

Norm pulled another face. "Can I remember
what you just **told** me, or can I remember what
you just told me actually **happening**?"

Ellie giggled. "You're funny."

For the second time in the space of half an hour, alarm bells began clanging loudly in Norm's head. Ellie thought that he was *funny*? And, according to Chelsea, women found funny guys *attractive*? Except that *Chelsea* didn't find *him* attractive. But what if ...

Norm's train of thought was abruptly derailed as Santa bounded over and jumped up, very nearly knocking him off his feet.

"Down, boy!" shouted Ellie.

Norm briefly considered asking Ellie if she was talking to the dog, or *him* – but decided not to, just in case

she found *that* funny, too. Or maybe she was just one of those really annoying people who thought that *everything* was funny? Not that Norm could imagine what *that* would be like. He was lucky if he laughed once a *day*. And that was usually only if one of his brothers had fallen over and hurt themselves. Or if they'd bumped into something and hurt themselves. Norm didn't care which.

As long as one of them ended up crying. But right now it didn't matter, anyway. What Norm was much more concerned about was the fact that he'd got an even smellier dog than John bouncing up and down in front of him like some kind of mad, dribbling pogo stick.

"I think he likes you," said Ellie.

Gordon flipping **Bennet,** thought Norm. Not the dog too?

WOOF WOOF! went Santa.

"He says, **thank you**," said Ellie.

"Really?" said Norm. "You can tell?"

"Of course," said Ellie, with a laugh.

"Just sounded like a dog going **woof**, to me."

Ellie laughed again. "Seriously, though. He definitely likes you, Norman."

Norm shrugged. "Maybe he can just smell John."

"John?" said Ellie.

Norm nodded. "Our dog."

"Oh," said Ellie.

"Well, I say **our** dog," said Norm. "He's my brothers' dog, really."

"What kind is it?" said Ellie.

"Cockapoo."

"Ah, sweet," said Ellie. "Santa's a shih tzu."

"Pardon?" said Norm.

"Santa," said Ellie. "He's a shih tzu. But you probably knew that already."

"What?" said Norm. "Er, no."

"Why did you call your dog John?"

"I didn't," said Norm.

"But I thought you just said ..."

"My brothers called him John," said Norm. "After my grandpa's favourite member of the Beatles. John McCartney."

"Lennon," said Ellie.

"What?" said Norm.

"It's John **Lennon**. Not McCartney."

"Whatever," said Norm. "Why did you call **your** dog Santa?"

"It's an anagram."

Norm looked puzzled. "I thought you said it was a shih tzu."

"**He**," said Ellie. "Not **it**. And he **is**."

"What?" said Norm.

"His **name**'s an anagram. You know? When you can make a word from the letters of another word?"

"Oh, right," said Norm. "So what's it an anagram of, then?"

"Satan," said Ellie matter-of-factly.

"**Satan?**" said Norm.

"Think about it."

Norm thought about it. And he had to admit, it wasn't exactly the answer he'd been expecting. But whatever. He didn't particularly care, anyway. He was just making conversation until he could get back on his bike and set off again. It had seemed only polite to ask, after Ellie had asked **him**.

But now that he had?

"Why didn't you just call him Satan?"

"My parents didn't think it was appropriate."

"I dunno," said Norm. "Parents, eh?"

Ellie suddenly burst out laughing. "Stop it! You're going to make me wet myself in a minute!"

Whoa, thought Norm. This was **way** too much information. And besides, he was starting to get **seriously** annoyed. He hadn't even **meant** that to be funny. He'd just said it for something to **say**. Why did everyone find him **so** flipping hilarious?

Maybe he was wasting his time trying to become World Mountain Biking Champion? Perhaps he'd be better off trying to become a comedian, instead? An actual comedian on the TV. Not just someone who could make their friends and

family laugh. Maybe there was actual *money* to be made out of being funny.

"Are your mum and dad funny?" said Ellie, once she'd calmed down enough to be able to speak again.

Were his parents *funny*? thought Norm. They were about as funny as getting a puncture in the middle of nowhere and not having a flipping puncture repair kit. In fact, getting a puncture in the middle of nowhere and not having a puncture repair kit would actually be *funnier* than his flipping *parents*. That's how *un*funny *they* were.

"I'm just wondering who you take after," said Ellie. "Your mum or your dad?"

Norm shuddered. He didn't like to think he took after **either** of his parents in any way whatso-flipping-**ever**. He certainly **hoped** he didn't, anyway. Did he actually **have** to take after one of them, just because they were biologically related? Or **allegedly** biologically related, anyway. Why did he have to take after **anyone** in his own family? Why couldn't he take after a badger, instead?

"Maybe you're just naturally funny," said Ellie.

Norm sighed. "Yeah, maybe."

"Have you done that homework yet, by the way?" said Ellie.

Norm looked confused. "What homework?"

"Seriously?" said Ellie.

"Seriously," said Norm.

"The **geography** homework?" said Ellie. "Don't tell me you've forgotten already?"

All right then, thought Norm. He **wouldn't** tell her that he'd forgotten already. Even though he obviously **had** forgotten. And anyway, even if he **had** remembered the homework, how **could** he have done it already? It was only about three seconds since he'd **last** seen Ellie. All he'd done was get home, shovel his tea down his neck, been annoyed by Chelsea and fall off his bike to avoid hitting a flipping anagram. Well, jump off it, anyway. But that wasn't the point. The point was that it would have been almost flipping **impossible** to do his homework in that short space of time. What did Ellie think he **was**? Some kind of nerdy freak of nature?

"I'll take that as a **yes**, then?" said Ellie.

"What?" said Norm.

"You've forgotten about the homework? Again?"

"Kind of."

Ellie smiled. "***Kind*** of?"

Norm ***almost*** smiled himself. But not quite.

"Do you even ***know*** what it is?" asked Ellie.

"Know what ***what*** is?"

"The ***homework***!"

Uh? thought Norm. How was he supposed to know what the homework actually ***was*** when he didn't even know he'd ***got*** flipping homework in the ***first*** flipping place? That made about as much sense as drying himself ***before*** he got in the flipping bath.

"I'll take that as a **no**, then," said Ellie.

Norm sighed. He didn't care how, when or **where** she took it. Not only that, but he didn't care whether she actually **told** him what the flipping homework was or not. But if she **was** going to tell him, he wished she'd just flipping hurry up and not keep him in suspense, like this was some stupid **book** or something. Because the sooner she told him, the sooner he could get back on his bike and head for the hills. Well, head for the **hill**, anyway. If you could actually **call** the hill behind the precinct a flipping hill. Frankly, Norm had  seen bigger goose bumps. But it was the closest thing to a hill that **he** had to bike down and unless his dad suddenly got a job in the Himalayas or somewhere similar, it would have to do for now.

"Would you like me tell you?" said Ellie.

"Yes, please, that would be lovely," said Norm,

somehow managing to remain calm on the **outside**, even though on the **inside** he was bubbling away like some kind of out-of-control science experiment.

"OK, I will," said Ellie.

Gordon flipping **Bennet**, thought Norm, as he waited for her to go on. This was getting ridiculous. In fact, never mind **getting** ridiculous. It had already **got** ridiculous! Was Ellie **ever** going to say what this flipping geography homework actually **was**? This wasn't just **frustrating**. This was pure **torture**!

"I tell you what," said Ellie. "I'll just message you on Facebook instead. It's probably easier."

Easier? thought Norm. Easier than **what**?

Bricklaying?

Tightrope walking?
Juggling fish? Why
couldn't she just
flipping **say** it and
put him out of his
misery?

On the other hand,
thought Norm,
at least if Ellie
did message
him, it would
mean getting
away just that **little**
bit earlier. And with the
sun rapidly disappearing
behind the so-called
hill, every second was
going to count.

"That OK?" said Ellie.

"Whatever," said Norm,
picking up his bike.

WOOF! WOOF! went Santa.

"Santa says 'Take care'!" said Ellie.

"Really?" said Norm, turning around. "Sounded just the same as 'thank you' to **me**."

Ellie laughed. "You are **so** funny, Norman!"

Gordon flipping **Bennet**, thought Norm, getting on his bike and setting off again. What was so funny about **that**? Still. It could've been worse. At least Ellie pronounced his name right.

CHAPTER 7

Norm shot off through the precinct and towards the woods like a rat up a drainpipe. But he hadn't pedalled more than fifty metres before he suddenly had to jam his brakes on again and skid to a halt.

"Well, blow me down if it isn't my **least** favourite grandson," said Grandpa, emerging from the supermarket, a carrier bag in each hand.

"Hi, Grandpa," mumbled Norm.

"No offence, by the way, Norman."

"None taken," said Norm. "I know you're only joking."

"Or am I?" said Grandpa.

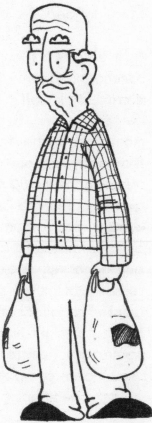

They looked at each other for a moment before Grandpa's eyes crinkled ever so slightly in the corners. Which was the closest Grandpa ever came to smiling.

"Well?" said Grandpa.

"Well?" said Norm.

"Fancy bumping into **you** here."

"Yeah," said Norm. "Fancy."

"Or **almost** bumping into you, anyway. You practising for the *Tour de France* or something?"

"What?" said Norm.

"That was a heck of a speed you were doing."

Norm nodded. "Yeah."

"Is it a bird? Is it a plane?" said Grandpa in an American accent. "No! It's just Norman on his bike!"

Norm sighed. If he'd actually *needed* confirmation that today was 'one of those days', *this* was it. Not that he actually *did* need it. And not that he wasn't glad to bump into Grandpa, of course. Norm was *always* glad to bump into Grandpa. Well, *nearly* always. It was just that there was no such thing as a quick chat with Grandpa. And Norm had already sensed that this was going to be anything *but* a quick chat. In fact, at *this* rate, thought Norm, he might have to nip back home and get his toothbrush and a flipping sleeping bag.

Which would have been fine if he'd been **deliberately** trying to avoid doing something, or **deliberately** trying to waste time. In those circumstances, Norm would have quite happily chatted with Grandpa till the flipping cows came home. Not today, though. Not with it getting darker by the second. And anyway, thought Norm, it wasn't **that** much of a coincidence bumping into Grandpa, was it? They only lived a few **streets** apart. It wasn't like they lived on separate **continents**, or anything. They were **bound** to bump into each other **once** in a while. What was the big deal?

"So where's the fire?" said Grandpa.

"What?"

"Where's the fire?"

"What fire?" said Norm.

Grandpa looked at Norm for a moment. "There isn't one."

Uh? thought Norm. So what was the flipping point of **saying** that, then? Was this some kind of **joke**? Because if so, he didn't get it. Grandpa might as well have asked where the flipping **volcano** was. Because there wasn't one of **those** around here either.

"Not an **actual** fire," said Grandpa.

"Uh?" said Norm, none the wiser.

"It's just an **expression**."

"Right," said Norm.

"It means, what's the hurry?"

"Right," said Norm again, even though he still didn't really know what Grandpa was on about.

"So?" said Grandpa, raising his cloud-like eyebrows.

"So?" said Norm.

"Are you going to **tell** me, or am I going to have to guess?"

"Guess what?"

"What the **hurry** is?"

"Oh, **right**!" said Norm, the penny **finally** dropping. "Erm, I just need to get to the woods, Grandpa."

"Why?"

"'Cos I want to go **biking** there."

"Of course," said Grandpa. "Silly me. I might have known it had something to do with **biking**."

"Yeah," said Norm.

"You and your biking, eh, Norman?"

"Yeah, I know," said Norm, wondering at what point it would be safe to assume that the conversation was finally at an end and he could set off again without appearing rude. Not that it had been much of a conversation. Grandpa had done most of the talking so far. And Norm got the distinct impression that, given the opportunity, Grandpa would be perfectly happy to go on talking for a good while yet.

"Have you any idea how old those woods **are**, Norman?"

Gordon flipping **Bennet**, thought Norm. This was no time for a flipping **history** lesson. If there actually **was** such a thing as a good time for a flipping **history** lesson. And in Norm's opinion there **wasn't**.

"I'll tell you, shall I?"

"'Kay," said Norm, despite not having a flipping **clue** where all this was leading, or what the point of it was. If indeed there actually **was** a point. Maybe the whole point was that there **wasn't** a point. Whatever, thought Norm. But Grandpa had started now, so he might as well let him finish.

"Those trees have stood there for several centuries," said Grandpa.

Yeah, thought Norm. He was beginning to know how they flipping **felt**.

"They'll still be here tomorrow," said Grandpa. "And the day after that. And the day after that. And the day after that."

Norm was struggling to see what this had to do with anything. If, in fact, it had **anything** to do with anything. Which seemed doubtful.

"So what's the **rush**, Norman?"

"What?" said Norm.

"Slow **down**," said Grandpa.

Slow **down**? thought Norm. How could he slow down? He was already **stopped**. If he went any **slower** he'd be going **backwards**.

"Why do you need to go right **now**?" asked Grandpa.

Norm pulled a face. "Because it's going to be dark

in a minute and I won't be able to see where I'm going."

"Oh, right, fair enough," said Grandpa. "In that case I'd better not keep you."

Norm sighed. It was too late for **that**. Grandpa had **already** kept him. If he was **lucky** he might get five minutes of biking in before it was pitch black in the woods. Ten minutes tops. After that it would be way too dangerous. Not for **Norm**, but for his **bike**. Norm didn't mind sustaining the odd bit of damage to himself. If he did, he'd  have given up biking a long time ago and taken up something less risky instead. Like knitting. But what Norm **did** mind was his **bike** getting damaged. Because repairs were expensive. And there was no flipping chance of getting a new bike. Not until his dad got another job there wasn't, anyway. Or his mum started working more than three seconds a flipping week at the cake shop. Either way, it wasn't going to happen anytime **soon**.

Norm nearly jumped out of his skin as the Beatles suddenly started blasting out of Grandpa's coat pocket. Or rather, as a Beatles **ringtone** suddenly started blasting out of Grandpa's coat pocket. And not that Norm actually **knew** that it was the Beatles. As far as Norm was concerned, it was just someone singing about living in a yellow submarine.

Although why anyone would actually want to live in a yellow submarine, or any other colour of submarine for that matter, was beyond Norm's comprehension. But that wasn't the point. The point was that someone was ringing Grandpa.

"Hello?" said Grandpa eventually, after putting down one of his carrier bags and answering his phone. "Oh, hello, love."

Norm knew what **that** meant. It meant that it was his mum. **Norm's** mum. Not **Grandpa's** mum. That would have been ridiculous. **Grandpa's** mum had been dead for about 700 years.

"It's your mum," said Grandpa, looking at Norm.

Norm nodded. There didn't seem much point saying that he'd already managed to work that out for himself. It would only delay him even **_longer_**.

"What's that?" said Grandpa to Norm's mum. "No, I was talking to Norman."

Grandpa listened. "Yes, we bumped into each other at the precinct." Grandpa listened again. "I know. Fancy that, eh?"

Gordon flipping **_Bennet_**, thought Norm. Imagine if he and Grandpa ever **_did_** bump into each other on the other side of the flipping **_world_** or something. It would be headline news all over the planet.

"Tomorrow night?" said Grandpa.

"Hmm, let me see. What am I doing tomorrow night?"

Norm sighed. He knew what **he'd** be doing tomorrow night, if he wasn't careful. He'd still be standing here talking to Grandpa. Or *listening* to him, anyway.

"Baby-sitting?" said Grandpa. "No, that should be fine. See you then." Grandpa listened some more. "No problem, love. I'll tell him. Bye."

Norm watched as Grandpa ended the call and put his phone back in his coat pocket.

"Oh, well, I'd best get off, I suppose," said Grandpa. "This lasagne's not going to cook itself."

"But ..." began Norm.

"What?" said Grandpa.

"Weren't you supposed to be telling me something?"

"Oh, yes, so I was," said Grandpa. "Thanks for reminding me."

Norm shrugged. "Don't mention it."

"Memory like a sieve!" said Grandpa.

Norm looked at Grandpa expectantly. Was he actually going to tell him, or what? This was even more agonising than when he'd been talking to

Ellie a few minutes earlier!

"Erm, Grandpa?"

"What is it?"

"What did my mum ask you to tell me?"

"What?" said Grandpa. "Oh, sorry, yes. She said you've got to go home."

"Seriously?" said Norm. "Right *now*?"

Grandpa nodded. "Yes. She said it right now."

"Uh?" said Norm. "No, I know she *said* it right now, Grandpa. But did she mean I had to go *home* right now?"

"I'm afraid so," said Grandpa.

"Why?"

Grandpa frowned until his eyebrows very nearly met in the middle. "Why am I afraid so?"

"What?" said Norm. "No, Grandpa! Why have I got to go home right *now*?"

"Oh, I see," said Grandpa. "Because it's too dark."

Norm sighed. He knew it. He just flipping *knew* it. If it wasn't so monu-flipping-mentally unfair, it would *almost* have been funny. Yeah, he thought, turning his bike around until it was pointing in the direction he'd just come from. *Almost* funny. But not *quite*.

"See you tomorrow, then," said Grandpa.

"Yeah," said Norm, beginning to pedal. "See you tomorrow, Grandpa."

CHAPTER 8

By the time Norm turned into his drive and skidded to a halt precisely two millimetres from the garage door, it was **totally** dark. Or at least it **would** have been totally dark if it hadn't been for all the street lighting and light spilling out of neighbouring houses, and the headlights of passing vehicles. But if it hadn't been for all **that**, Norm wouldn't have

 been able to see beyond the end of his nose. Not that there was actually anything interesting or exciting to **see** beyond the end of his nose. And not that **that** was much consolation to Norm. Or **any** consolation to Norm, for that matter.

Because as far as **he** was concerned, he'd been deprived of an opportunity to do the **one** thing that he really **loved** doing. Biking.

OK, thought Norm, so it wasn't as though he could have done it for very **long**. It was **always** going to get dark at **some** point. It wasn't like it was going to stay light all night like it did at the flipping North Pole in the middle of summer. Or the **South** Pole in the middle of winter, or whatever. So he would have had to come back home **eventually**, worse flipping luck. But at least he'd have had the chance to zoom down a few trails and weave in and out of a few trees first.

And, yes, Grandpa was right. The trees wouldn't be going anywhere soon. Or at least, Norm **presumed** they wouldn't be going anywhere soon. They'd still be there the next day. And the next day. And the day after that. And the day after **that**.

But that wasn't the flipping point, as far as Norm was concerned. The point, as far as Norm was concerned, was that he **could** have gone biking. He **should** have gone biking. But he didn't. And it felt like daylight flipping robbery. As if **someone** had literally **stolen** all the light! It was **so** flipping annoying.

If there was **one** good thing about not being able to go biking because it was too dark – and there **was** only **one** thing that Norm could think of off the top of his head – it was that it was **also** too dark for Chelsea to be lurking around like a flipping vampire and popping up on the other side of the fence the second he appeared on the drive. At least he'd been spared **that**. So it wasn't **all** bad, thought Norm, closing the front door behind him. But it was still bad enough.

"Is that you, love?" called Norm's mum from the front room.

"No, it's a flipping burglar," mumbled Norm to himself.

"We're in the front room!"

Norm sighed. Not only did he already **know** that his mum was in the front room, but if he really **had** been a burglar he'd have been free to wander around the rest of the house and help himself to whatever he wanted, like one of those TV programmes where people whizzed around supermarkets filling up their trolleys. Not that there was anything worth burgling in **this** flipping house, thought Norm bitterly. He doubted they'd get more than fifty quid for everything put together, at a car boot sale. Maybe a hundred if you included the actual **house**. That's if anyone was stupid enough to buy it in the first place. And, frankly, if they did, they needed their flipping heads examining. And another thing, thought Norm. What was

that weird music they were listening to in there?

But if Norm thought the actual **music** was weird, it was **nothing** compared to the scene that greeted him when he walked into the front room. Because the scene that greeted Norm when he walked into the front room took **weird** to a whole new level. And not just **weird.** It was excruciatingly embarrassing. Not to mention hair-raisingly terrifying.

"What's the matter, love?" laughed Norm's mum. "You look like you've just seen a ghost!"

Norm almost wished he **had** seen a flipping ghost. It would have been a **lot** less scary than this. Then again, thought Norm, pretty much **anything** would have been less scary than **this**. Being pursued down the street by an army of zombiefied Chelsea clones would have been less scary than **this**.

It was like a scene from a horror movie that had been cut because it was just a bit **too** horrific. Not just **eighteen** rated. A **hundred** and eighteen rated.

"I know," said Norm's dad. "Anybody would think he'd never seen his parents dancing before!"

Dancing? thought Norm. Seriously? Was that **really** what it was? Because it didn't look much like dancing to **him**. Not that Norm was any kind of expert when it came to dancing. He knew more about keeping tropical **fish** than he knew about **dancing**.  And the only thing he knew about keeping tropical fish was that they preferred to be kept in **water**. But even so, Norm could see that whatever it was that his mum and dad were doing had very little, if **anything**, to do with **dancing**. Quite honestly it looked more like two snakes wrestling, to him. Not that Norm had ever actually **seen** two snakes wrestling before. But that wasn't the point. The point was that whatever his parents were doing shouldn't be allowed. In fact, not only should it not be allowed, it should be made flipping **_illegal_**.

His dad was right about **_one_** thing though, thought Norm. He **_hadn't_** ever seen his parents 'dancing'

 before. And, frankly, if that was what it looked like, he never wanted to see it again, either. But this wasn't something that Norm was likely to forget in a hurry. Or even forget **_slowly_**. Because once you'd seen something **_that_** shocking, it was very difficult to ever **_un_**see it.

Norm couldn't simply **_delete_** it from his memory when his brain got too full. This was something **_so_** traumatic it would haunt him for the rest of his life.

But if Norm thought that the sight of his mum and dad's so-called 'dancing' was as weird as things could get, he had another think coming. Because it was nothing compared to what happened **_next_**. In fact, compared to what happened **_next_**, Norm's mum and dad's so-called 'dancing' seemed like the most natural thing in the world, and hardly worth mentioning at all.

"Gordon flipping **_Bennet_**!" yelled Norm, as Brian and John suddenly pirouetted past. Or rather, Brian pirouetted past. John didn't appear to have a great deal of choice in the matter, what with Norm's middle brother holding his front paws up, leaving him only his **_back_** legs to stand on. And as if that still wasn't quite disturbing **_enough_**, John appeared to be wearing a spangly bow tie.

"Language!" hissed Dave.

"What?" said Norm, turning around to see his little brother holding an iPad in front of him.

"Ssssssh!" said Dave. "I'm trying to film!"

"Well, I didn't know that, did I?"

"Well, you do now," said Dave.

Norm pulled a face. "What are you doing *that* for, anyway?"

Dave shrugged. "Because it's funny?"

"Funny?" said Norm. "That's not *funny*, Dave. It's *disgusting*!"

"It's not disgusting," said Brian, as he and John pirouetted past again, in the opposite direction.

"Yeah, it is," said Norm.

"Is it because we're both **boys**?" said Brian.

"What?" said Norm. "No. 'Course it's not, you **doughnut**. It's because one of you's a flipping **dog**!"

"So?" said Brian defiantly.

"So that's flipping **disgusting**!" said Norm. "And **weird.**"

Brian looked genuinely surprised. "Weird?"

"Yeah," said Norm. "W. I. R. E. D. Weird."

"That spells 'wired'," said Dave, who by now had finished filming and was busy pressing buttons on the iPad.

"Shut up, you little freak!" spat Norm.

"Charming," said Dave.

"Anyway, we're just **dancing**," said Brian. "We're not doing anyone any **harm**."

"Yeah, you are," said Norm. "You're doing **me** harm by making me watch it."

"I'm not **making** you watch it," said Brian. "You don't **have** to watch it. You could watch the TV instead."

"What?" said Norm, getting louder and louder to try and make himself heard above the music. "How could I watch the TV with **that** flipping racket going on?"

"I didn't say anything about **listening** to the TV, did I?" said Brian. "I just said you could **watch** it. And, anyway, that's not a racket. It's salsa music!"

"WHAT?" yelled Norm.

"Salsa music," said Brian. "From Cuba."

"Uh?" said Norm. "Scuba?"

"**Cuba!**" said Brian.

Norm sighed. He didn't particularly care **where** the music came from. It could have come from flipping **Venus** as far as **he** was concerned. And why did Brian have to have an answer for **everything**? As if he wasn't quite annoying enough **already.**

"Anyway, that's not **dancing**!" said Norm.

"Well, what would **you** call it, then?" said Brian.

"Dunno," said Norm. "But whatever it is, it's flipping **wrong**."

"What's **wrong** with it?" said Brian, finally stopping and allowing John to stand on all fours again. Not that John actually stood on all fours again for very long, preferring instead to sit down on the floor and sniff his bottom.

Norm thought for a moment. What was **wrong** with his ridiculous ten-year-old doughnut of a brother twirling and whirling around the front room, dragging their flipping Cockapoo around with him like some kind of diseased, drooling **mop**? Where did he start? Where did he even **begin** to start? **Everything** was flipping wrong with it! There was nothing that **wasn't** wrong with it! Was he the **only** person here who couldn't actually **see** that? Was he the **only** person in the room who wasn't actually barking, flipping **mad**?

"Aw, you **like** it, don't you, boy?" said Brian in a funny, squeaky baby voice, bending over so that his nose was very nearly touching John's. "Yes, you do, don't you!"

WOOF! went John, before licking Brian full in the face.

"Aw, that is **so** gross!" said Norm.

"No, it's not," said Brian.

"He won't **catch** anything," said Dave.

"No," said Norm. "But the **dog** might."

"Ha, ha, Norman," said Brian. "You're so funny."

"Funny you should say that," said Norm.

"Say what?" said Brian.

"That I'm funny."

"Actually, I was being sarcastic," said Brian.

"Yeah, I know that, *actually*, Brian," said Norm. "But it was still funny."

"It's funny that Brian said you're *funny*?" said Dave. "Why's that?"

"Because everyone's been ..." began Norm. But that was as far as that particular sentence ever got. Because there was something that Norm had only just noticed. Something that Norm would have *normally* noticed a lot sooner if it hadn't been for everything else that had been going on, such as parents writhing like wrestling snakes and dogs in bow ties doing flipping scuba dancing or whatever.

"Everyone's been *what*?" said Dave.

"Is that my iPad?" said Norm, ignoring Dave's question.

"What?" said Dave.

"You heard," said Norm. "*Is* it?"

"Er, it might be," said Dave.

"What do you mean, it *might* be, Dave, you little freak?"

"Er, yeah, it is, actually."

Norm couldn't quite believe it. Even though he could *see* for himself that it was true.

"Who said you could use that?"

"Nobody," said Dave. "But ..."

"But what?" said Norm.

"Nobody said I *couldn't* use it."

"Seriously?" said Norm.

Dave shrugged. "Seriously."

"So unless someone tells you that you *can't* do something, you think it's OK to *do* it?"

"Pardon?" said Dave.

"Has anyone ever told you **not** to rob a bank?" said Norm.

"No," said Dave.

"Exactly!" said Norm. "Doesn't mean you can flipping **do** it, does it?"

"What?" said Dave.

"Has anyone ever told you **not** to bring a rhino into school?"

"No, but ..."

"Oh, I get it!" said Brian, joining in. "Has anyone ever told you not to taunt a crocodile, Dave?"

Dave pulled a face. "'Course they haven't."

"Exactly!" said Brian triumphantly. "Doesn't mean you should **do** it!"

Gordon flipping **Bennet**, thought Norm, wondering how much more of this he was going to be able to take.

"Have you ever stuck your finger up a lion's—"

"Brian?" said Norm, who had no wish to hear the end of that particular sentence. Or any other sentence from Brian for that matter.

"Yeah?" said Brian.

"Shut up!"

"*MUUUUUM! DAAAAAD!*"

wailed Brian at the top of his voice.

"What is it?" snapped Norm's mum, unable to

ignore the squabbling any longer and turning the music off.

"Norman just told me to shut up!"

"That's enough now!" said Norm's mum sternly.

"Yeah, Norman," smirked Brian.

"Both of you," said Norm's mum.

"Yeah, Brian," smirked Dave.

"*All* of you!" said Norm's dad, the vein on the side of his head beginning to throb.

"Time for bed, you two," said Norm's mum, pointing first at Brian and then at Dave.

"'Kay, Mum," said Brian, heading for the door.

"'Kay, Mum," said Dave, heading after him.

Little creeps, thought Norm.

"And Norman?"

"Yeah, Mum?" said Norm.

"Up to your room."

Gladly, thought Norm, following his brothers, only too happy and relieved to be able to escape the escalating mayhem and spend some time alone. There was something he needed to do first, though.

"Gimme that back, Dave," said Norm, when he reached the hall.

"What do you say?" said Dave, stopping and turning around halfway up the stairs.

"I'd say you've got about three seconds, you little freak," said Norm. "Three ... two ..."

"Help yourself," said Dave, putting the iPad down before Norm had the chance to get to 'one'.

"And next time, flipping **ask** first," said Norm.

But Dave had already disappeared. Not that there was actually going to **be** a next time as far as **Norm** was concerned.

CHAPTER 9

Norm barely had time to dive onto his bed and fire up his iPad before it pinged, alerting him that he'd received a new notification. Which was odd for a start, thought Norm, plumping up his pillow and getting comfy, because he hadn't been in touch with anyone recently and wasn't expecting to **hear** from anyone, either.

Of course, there was always the possibility that someone might have just been randomly getting in touch, thought Norm, clicking on the notifications icon. That was the beauty of Facebook and all that stuff. **Anybody** could get in touch with **anybody**. **Whenever** they wanted. Then again, the only person that Norm ever communicated with on a regular basis was Mikey. And, as far as Norm knew, Mikey was probably still busy practising whatever it was that he was supposed to be practising. And besides, Mikey usually just phoned or texted if he wanted to get hold of Norm to chat or whatever.

Norm pulled a face as he stared at the screen. Someone had 'liked' a video he'd posted? Who? But, more importantly, **what** flipping video? Because Norm hadn't posted any videos lately.  Not as far as he could remember he hadn't, anyway. Which admittedly wasn't **all** that far. Norm could only just about remember coming up the flipping stairs just now, let alone whether he'd posted a flipping video on Facebook or not.

A couple of clicks later and Norm was watching the video that **he'd** posted. Or rather, the video that he clearly **hadn't** posted. Because if Norm ever posted or shared anything whatsoever on social media, there was a 99 per cent chance of it having at least **something** to do with biking. In fact, never mind a 99 per cent chance. It abso-flipping-lutely **would** have something to do with biking. 100 per cent.

No question about it. As for the chances of Norm ever posting a so-called 'funny' animal video? There was more chance of ... Well, there was more chance of just about **anything** happening than there was of Norm ever doing **that**. Even **less** chance of him ever posting a video of Brian and John, so-called **dancing** together.

"DAVE?"

bawled Norm furiously at full volume. Not that there was

154

actually any need for Norm to bawl at all, what with the wall separating **his** room from his brothers' being no thicker than flipping toilet paper and slightly less soundproof. He could have spoken at a perfectly **normal** volume and Dave would have still heard him. In fact, never mind **talking**, thought Norm, he could have probably just flipping **thought** really loudly and Dave would **still** have heard him.

"What is it?" said Dave, appearing in Norm's doorway a few moments later.

"What do you mean, 'What is it?'" said Norm, looking up.

Dave shrugged. He genuinely didn't seem to know why he'd been suddenly summoned to Norm's room. Or, at least, if he **did**, he was doing a pretty good job of **pretending** that he didn't know why.

"Seriously?" said Norm.

Dave nodded. "Seriously."

Norm sighed and raised the iPad a little bit higher. "What do you call this?"

"An iPad?" said Dave uncertainly, as if this might be some kind of trick question.

Norm looked at his little brother for a moment. He was doing his best to keep reasonably calm. But Dave wasn't making it very easy for him. "I **know** it's a flipping iPad, Dave, you **doughnut**. It's **my** flipping iPad."

"Excellent," said Dave, heading off again. "Glad we've got that sorted."

"Oi, come back here!" said Norm.

"What's the problem?" said Dave, reappearing in the doorway.

Norm sighed again. "The **problem**, Dave, is **this**."

"What?" said Dave.

"**This**," said Norm, jabbing the iPad screen repeatedly with one of his index fingers.

jab jab
jab
jab
jab

"**What?**" said Dave.

"Don't just flipping **stand** there, Dave! Come and flipping **look**!" snapped Norm, hitting the play button again.

Dave did as he was told and wandered over to see what all the fuss was about. "Oh, **that**!" He laughed as Brian and John pirouetted into view on the screen.

Norm looked at Dave in disbelief. "What do you mean, 'Oh, that'?"

"It's good, isn't it?" giggled Dave. "Ooh, look. Someone's 'liked' it already!"

There was a sudden ping from the iPad. Followed by another. And another. And another.

"Ooh, that's five 'likes' now!" squeaked Dave excitedly. "It's going viral!"

"What?" said Norm.

"Brilliant!" said Dave.

"Brilliant?" said Norm, screwing his face up in consternation.

"Yeah," said Dave. "Why? Don't **you** think it's brilliant, Norman?"

"Er, no, I **don't**, actually," said Norm.

"Really?" said Dave. "Why not?"

"Why **not**?" said Norm, as if Dave had just asked why stuff fell **down**, instead of **up**.

"Yeah," said Dave.

"I'll tell you why **not**!" said Norm. "Because you shouldn't have been on my flipping **Facebook** in the first flipping place! That's why **not**, Dave!"

"Yeah, but ..."

"Yeah but, no but, Dave! How did you even know my password?"

Dave shrugged. "It's not rocket science."

"I know it's not **rocket science**, Dave," said Norm. "That would be a **stupid** password."

"What?" said Dave. "No, I mean it wasn't hard to guess your password."

Norm looked at Dave for a moment. "You **guessed** my password?"

"Yeah."

Norm sighed. "Gordon flipping Bennet."

"Exactly," said Dave.

"What?" said Norm.

"Well, that's your password, isn't it?" said Dave. "'Gordon flipping Bennet.' It was the first thing I tried."

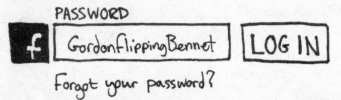

PASSWORD

f GordonflippingBennet   LOG IN

Forgot your password?

"Oh, right," said Norm.

"I told you," said Dave. "It's not rocket science."

Maybe not, thought Norm. But that wasn't the point. The point was that Dave still shouldn't have been on **his** flipping Facebook. There might have been stuff on there that he didn't want anyone else to see. OK, so there wasn't. It was mainly just stuff about bikes and biking. But that wasn't the point, either. There **might** have been. It was **his** Facebook and it was flipping **private**. And just because Dave had correctly guessed his password didn't mean he had the right to post stupid videos. It was like his pants drawer, thought Norm. Just because someone knew **how** to open it, didn't mean they flipping well **should** open it!

"What was I supposed to do?" said Dave.

"What do you **mean**, what were you supposed to do?" said Norm.

"Well, I'm too young to have my **own** Facebook," said Dave.

"Yeah, well, tough," said Norm.

"It's not fair," said Dave.

"Welcome to my **world**, Dave."

Dave grinned. "The world of Norman. Population, one."

"Yeah, whatever," said Norm, as his iPad pinged three more times.

"Who's Ellie?" said Dave, leaning over and peering at the screen.

"Don't be so flipping **nosy**, Dave!" said Norm, clutching the tablet to his chest.

"Is she your **girlfriend**?"

"What?" said Norm.

"Ellie," said Dave. "Is that your girlfriend?"

"'Course she's not, you **doughnut**," said Norm. "I don't even **have** a flipping girlfriend!"

"So how come you've gone red, then?"

"What are you **on** about, Dave? I haven't gone **red**!"

But even as Norm said it, he could tell that he **had** gone red. Which was annoying for a start. Because he **didn't** have a girlfriend. What did **he** want a flipping **girlfriend** for? Not that there was anything wrong with **girls**. Well, apart from Chelsea. But apart from **her**, Norm didn't have anything against girls. They were all right. Same as zebras were all right. Didn't mean Norm was going to go **out** with one, though.

"Well, whoever she is, she's sent you a message," said Dave.

"What?" said Norm, looking at his iPad again. "Oh, yeah."

Dave looked expectantly at Norm. "Well? What is it?"

"Uh?" said Norm. "Mind your own flipping *business*, Dave!"

"Charming," said Dave. "Can I go now?"

"Yeah, you can go now," said Norm, opening up the message. The message that Ellie had sent him. Ellie who most definitely *wasn't* his girlfriend.

"Bye, then," said Dave, disappearing again.

But Norm wasn't even listening any more. He was too busy staring at the jumble of nonsensical words on his iPad screen. Words which *apparently* spelled out the geography homework that he'd forgotten all about again and that he hadn't even known he'd had in the first place. But the words

may as well have been in Ancient Greek as far as Norm was concerned. In fact, if they **had** been in Ancient Greek there was more chance that Norm would have understood what the question actually **meant**. As it was, he had no idea whatso-flipping-**ever** what the question meant, let alone how on earth he was ever going to **answer** it.

"Gordon flipping **Bennet**," muttered Norm, as the iPad pinged three more times.

CHAPTER 10

By the time Norm went to bed that night, he'd somehow managed to forget all about the homework again. By the time he woke up the following **morning**, it was as if he'd never received the message from Ellie in the first place, let alone actually clicked on it and read it. The homework wasn't merely a **distant** memory, it was a memory from a different galaxy altogether. A galaxy far, far away. It was almost as if the memory had never existed at all. And, as far as Norm was concerned, it might as well **not** have existed. Because as far as **Norm** was concerned, Saturdays were about one thing and one thing only. Biking.

In a galaxy
far far away...
HOMEWORK

It didn't take long for Norm to get lost in his thoughts as he zoomed towards the precinct, where he and Mikey had arranged to meet before heading off to the woods together. Or rather, where they'd arranged to **rendezvous**, as Mikey had insisted on calling it, when they'd texted each other after breakfast. Quite why Mikey had to use fancy big words like **that** was a mystery to Norm. Then again, a **lot** of things were a mystery to Norm. But at least Mikey was going to be allowed out this time. And at least it was going to be light enough to ride. And at least the trees would still be there. Or at least Norm **hoped** they would be, anyway. Although knowing **his** flipping luck someone would have chopped them all down and built a flipping car park by now.

"Hi, Norman!" said a voice, just as Norm was whizzing past the supermarket.

"Uh? What?" said Norm, skidding to a halt before turning around to see Ellie walking towards him, together with Santa the shih tzu. "Oh, hi."

Ellie smiled. "So you know who I **am**, then?"

"What?" said Norm. "Yeah, 'course I do."

WOOF! went Santa.

"Santa says hi, too," said Ellie.

Gordon flipping **Bennet**, thought Norm. She didn't honestly expect him to believe **that**, did she? That her dog had actually just said 'Hi'? How could she **tell**? It had just flipping **barked**, that was all. Just like John or any other flipping dog did. It could have been saying  literally **anything**. Or **trying** to, anyway. Then again, it **could** have just been barking. Because it was a flipping **dog**. And dogs didn't **talk**. At least, not in **real** life they didn't, anyway.

"Aren't you going to say hi back?"

"What?" said Norm.

"To Santa?" said Ellie. "It's only polite."

Norm sighed. "Hi, Santa."

"There," said Ellie. "That wasn't so hard, was it?"

No, thought Norm. Just flipping *stupid*.

WOOF! went Santa again, before licking Norm's hand enthusiastically. A bit *too* enthusiastically as far as Norm was concerned.

Ellie giggled. "He definitely likes *you*, Norman!"

"You think so?" said Norm, pulling a face. Partly because he was pretty grossed out at being treated like some kind of human lollipop. But mainly because if Santa really *did* like him, it was a pretty weird way of *showing* it. The only consolation, thought Norm, was that humans didn't go around licking each other. Because that really *would* be gross.

"So," said Ellie.

"So," said Norm. But only because he couldn't think what else to say.

"Fancy bumping into **you** here."

"Yeah, fancy," said Norm. But only because he still couldn't think what else to say. And, anyway, rather like the previous evening when he'd seen Grandpa here in the precinct, it really wasn't **that** big a deal. It wasn't like they'd met on the moon, or something.

"Well, not **literally** bumping into you," said Ellie. "Not like last time, eh? Well, not like **nearly** last time, anyway."

"What?" said Norm. It was as though Ellie was talking in some kind of secret code. A code that **Norm** had **no** idea how to decipher.

"Well, I mean we didn't **actually** bump into each other last time, did we? We **nearly** did, but then you swerved heroically and decided to fall off your bike instead."

Norm sighed again. Did he **look** like someone who had nothing better to do than hang around shopping precincts talking to girls he hardly flipping knew? Or rather, being talked **at** by girls he hardly flipping knew? Because this was beginning to get on his flipping **nerves**. And anyway, he hadn't exactly **decided** to fall off his bike. It wasn't like he'd **wanted** to fall off his bike. It had just seemed like the most sensible option at the time given that he had been heading straight towards a flipping concrete rubbish bin!

"Apart from **that**, it's like, whoa! Déjà vu!" said Ellie.

"Déjà **who**?" said Norm.

"Not déjà **who**, Norman!" laughed Ellie. "Déjà **vu**! When you get a weird feeling that you've been in a certain situation before?"

"Right," said Norm, who was **definitely** beginning

to feel that he'd been in **this** situation before. And he had no intention of being in it for much longer, if he could possibly help it.

"You're so **funny**," said Ellie.

Here we go again, thought Norm. Why did people keep **saying** that? He hadn't been **trying** to be funny. He never **did** try to be funny. What did they think he **was**? A flipping **clown** or something? Because this wasn't just **annoying** now. It was **beyond** annoying. Way **beyond**. It was ...

"I like that video, by the way," said Ellie, before Norm had a chance to think what it was. Which was pretty annoying in itself.

"What video?" said Norm irritably.

"Your dog doing salsa? With your brother?"

WOOF! went Santa.

"That's right, Santa," said Ellie. "You liked it too, didn't you?"

WOOF! WOOF! went Santa.

"Gordon flipping **Bennet**," muttered Norm.

Ellie looked puzzled. "What's wrong with that?"

"I didn't post it," said Norm. "My brother did."

"Oh, I see," said Ellie. "Doesn't matter who posted it. It's still funny."

"You think?" said Norm.

"Don't *you*?" said Ellie.

"No, I don't, actually," said Norm.

"Well, *I* do, Norman. And so do at least three hundred others."

"What?" said Norm.

"That's how many likes it's got," said Ellie. "Well, that's how many it had when *I* looked at it before I came out. It's probably got loads more by now."

Norm couldn't believe it. How could that many people have seen the flipping video already? It was ridiculous. And what was even ***more*** ridiculous was the fact that they'd actually ***liked*** it. Hadn't they got ***better*** things to do? Like watch ***biking*** videos instead?

"Why didn't you delete it?" said Ellie.

"What?" said Norm.

"You could have just deleted it if you were ***that*** bothered about it."

"Yeah, well, I was going to, wasn't I?"

"So why didn't you?"

Norm shrugged. "I forgot."

"Why doesn't that surprise me?" Ellie grinned.

"Why doesn't **what** surprise you?"

"You forgetting to do something," said Ellie. "Talking of which ..."

"Talking of **what**?" said Norm, getting more confused by the second.

"Forgetting," said Ellie.

"Uh?" said Norm. "Forgetting **what**?"

Ellie looked at Norm for a moment. "You're **joking**, right?"

"I'm **not** joking!" said Norm. "Forgetting what?"

"The **geography** homework?" said Ellie.

"Oh, right," said Norm. "That."

"Yes, **that**!" laughed Ellie. But this time the laugh

sounded slightly forced, as if she was beginning to find Norm not *quite* so hilarious after all. Not that Norm noticed.

"What about it?" said Norm.

Ellie sighed wearily. "Have you actually *done* it yet?"

Norm shook his head. "Nah, not yet."

"Norman!" said Ellie.

"What?" said Norm. "It's not *my* fault!"

"Well, it's not *mine*, either!" said Ellie.

"You only sent me the message last night!"

"Yes, I know I did," said Ellie. "And if you'd been paying more attention in class, I wouldn't have *had* to send you a message in the first place, would I?"

"Dunno," said Norm with a shrug. "Anyway, I've got loads of time yet. It's only Saturday!"

"I'm perfectly aware what day it is," said Ellie.

Norm sighed.

"What is it?" said Ellie.

"I don't even know what the question **means**."

"It's perfectly straight-forward, Norman."

Yeah, thought Norm. To a flipping **geek**, maybe. To someone whose idea of a good time was flicking through an encyclo-flipping-**pedia**. Not to him it wasn't, though. It was about as straightforward as an instruction manual for a washing machine. In Swahili. Not that Norm had ever actually **read** an instruction manual for a washing machine in Swahili before. Or any **other** language for that matter.

"Just look at your notes," said Ellie.

"What?" said Norm, as if Ellie had just told him to look at the back of his own head.

"Don't tell me you forgot to take **notes** as well, Norman?"

"OK," said Norm.

"OK what?" said Ellie.

"I won't tell you I forgot to take notes."

Ellie looked at Norm and shook her head. "I don't know ..."

"That makes two of us, then," said Norm.

"And you're welcome, by the way," said Ellie.

"Uh?" said Norm. "What for?"

"For sending you the message."

"Oh, right," said Norm. "Yeah, thanks."

"And for reminding you about it in the first place," said Ellie.

Whatever, thought Norm. What did she want? A flipping **medal**, or something?

"If it hadn't been for me, you'd be in **big** trouble."

Big trouble? thought Norm. He doubted he'd be in **big** trouble. It wasn't exactly the end of the **world** to forget to do your flipping **homework**, was it? At least not for **Norm** it wasn't, anyway. Not in the great scheme of things. In fact, in the great scheme of things, thought Norm, forgetting to do your homework was really quite trivial and relatively unimportant. It wasn't like he'd accidentally blown up the science lab and destroyed the entire school, was it? He could see how **that** might upset one or two people. Not him **personally**, thought Norm. But

that wasn't the point. The point was that forgetting to do your homework really wasn't that big a deal at all. So how come Ellie was making such a song and flipping dance about it?

"So, I figure you probably owe me one," said Ellie.

Norm pulled a face.
"One what?"

"Favour," said Ellie.

"But …"

"But nothing, Norman. I've done **you** a huge favour and now you can do one for **me.** That's the way the cookie crumbles."

"Uh?" said Norm.

"It's one of my grandma's expressions," said Ellie.

"How many grandmas have you **got**?" asked Norm.

"Pardon?" said Ellie. "No, I mean my grandma says 'that's the way the cookie crumbles'. It means that's just the way it goes. You scratch my back, I scratch yours. That's another one of hers."

Norm sighed. What **was** it with old people and weird expressions? Grandpa had one for just about every possible occasion. Or at least it **seemed** like he did, anyway. As for him and Ellie scratching each other's backs? That was an image he'd prefer not to think about at that particular moment. Or ever, actually.

"What are you doing tonight?" asked Ellie.

The question stopped Norm dead in his tracks. Or

at least it **would** have done if he'd actually been **making** any tracks. And right now, Norm wished he flipping well **was** making tracks. With his bike. Preferably in the woods. But, frankly, **anywhere** else would do. And as quickly as possible.

"Well?" said Ellie.

"Erm ... I'm ... I don't think I'm ..."

"Doing anything?" interjected Ellie hopefully. "Excellent. In that case, you can be round at my place at seven."

WOOF! went Santa.

"What's that, boy?" said Ellie, turning her attention back to her dog.

WOOF! went Santa. WOOF, WOOF, WOOF!

"Oh, don't worry about **that**," said Ellie. "Norman already knows where we live, don't you, Norman?"

"What?" said Norm. "Er, yeah, I do."

Ellie smiled. "And you can always use your phone if you get lost."

Norm **tried** to muster up a smile too, but somehow the signal from his brain to his mouth didn't quite make it.

"So, is that a **deal**, then?"

"Erm, I'm not ..." began Norm.

"Brilliant," said Ellie. "Oh, hi, Mikey!"

Norm spun round to see his best friend cycling towards them. And just in the nick of time too, as far as Norm was concerned. Because goodness knows what Ellie would ask **next**.

"Hi, Mikey," said Norm.

"Hi," said Mikey, stopping and exchanging a sheepish glance with Ellie. Not that Norm noticed. But then, Norm wouldn't have noticed if it had suddenly started raining Coco Pops. **Proper** Coco Pops. Not just the cheapo supermarket own-brand variety. Because all **Norm** could think about right now was the fact that he seemed to have just agreed to be round  at Ellie's house for 7 o'clock that night. But **why** had he? How had that actually **happened**? And, perhaps more importantly, what exactly did Ellie have in mind? But now wasn't the time to ask. Not with Mikey having just shown up.

"Ready?" said Mikey.

Norm hesitated. "You talking to me, Mikey?"

"What?" said Mikey, after shooting another quick glance at Ellie. "Yeah, course I'm talking to you, Norm, you doughnut!"

"Just checking," said Norm. "And who are you calling a **doughnut**, by the way?"

"You, you doughnut," said Mikey.

"No, **you're** a doughnut," said Norm.

"No, **you're** a doughnut," said Mikey.

"No, **you're** a doughnut," said Norm.

"I'll leave you guys to it," said Ellie, setting off with Santa trotting happily beside her.

"'Kay, bye," called Mikey.

"Yeah, bye," called Norm.

"See you later!" called Ellie.

WOOF! went Santa.

"Santa says bye, too!"

But for once Norm wasn't bothered by Ellie's apparent ability to understand everything that her dog was saying. What Norm was **bothered** about was how much of **his** conversation with Ellie, **Mikey** had understood.

"What are you doing later, Norm?"

"Uh?" said Norm.

"With Ellie?"

"What do you mean?" said Norm.

"She said 'See you later'?"

"Yeah, so?" shrugged Norm. "People say that all the time, don't they? Even if you're not actually **going** to see them. It's like, you know? An expression?"

Mikey thought for a moment. "Suppose so."

"Anyway, how do you know she was talking to me?" said Norm.

"What?" said Mikey.

"She might have been talking to you."

"Suppose so," said Mikey again, setting off towards the woods. "Come on. Let's go, Norm."

Abso-flipping-***lutely***, thought Norm, pedalling after his friend before things could get any ***more*** awkward.

CHAPTER 11

"What's a deal?" said Mikey, as Norm caught up with him, just as they were passing the library. Not that Norm noticed where they were passing. Then again, Norm wouldn't have noticed if they'd been passing a second-hand cheese shop staffed entirely by mice. All **Norm** cared about was that he was **finally** going biking. And not a second too flipping soon, either.

"Norm?" said Mikey, when Norm showed no sign of replying.

"Yeah?" said Norm absent-mindedly, as though he'd been thinking of something else. Which he had.

"I said, what's a deal?"

Norm pulled a face. "What do you mean, what's a deal? A deal's like when you do something for somebody and then that somebody does something for **you** in return."

"I **know** what a **deal** is, Norm, you doughnut!" said Mikey.

"Uh?" said Norm. "So why flipping **ask**, then? You even **bigger** doughnut!"

"I **meant**, what's the deal you and Ellie just made?"

"What?" said Norm, trying not to immediately start panicking. After all, it was an innocent-enough question. Perhaps Mikey was just making idle chitchat.

"I heard her saying something about a deal, just now. And then she suddenly stopped when she saw me."

Norm shrugged nonchalantly. Or at least he **tried** to shrug nonchalantly. But shrugging wasn't easy when you were riding a bike. Nonchalantly, or otherwise.

"Maybe it was just a coincidence that she stopped when she saw you, Mikey."

"What do you mean?"

"Maybe she'd finished talking anyway."

"Hmmm. Maybe," said Mikey, sounding less than convinced. "So, what was it?"

"Uh?" said Norm.

"The **deal**?" said Mikey. "What was it?"

"I'm not **telling** you."

"Why not?" said Mikey.

"What do you mean, why **not**?" said Norm. "Because I just don't flipping **want** to, Mikey, **that's** why not! I don't have to tell you **everything**!"

"Fair enough," said Mikey.

"Flipping right it's fair enough," said Norm, not even sure **why** he was reluctant to tell Mikey about agreeing to go round to Ellie's later. All he knew was that he had a feeling in his gut that he just didn't **want** to tell him. Either that or it was wind.

"I just wondered, that's all," said Mikey.

"Yeah, well," said Norm.

"It's no biggie," said Mikey.

"You're right," said Norm. "It's not."

They rode on in silence for a few more seconds and had almost reached the end of the precinct before Mikey spoke again.

"Do you think you might tell me *later*?" he said tentatively.

"No, I flipping well—WHOOOOOOOAH!!!!" yelled Norm, swerving and only narrowly avoiding hitting the very same concrete rubbish bin he'd only

narrowly avoided hitting the previous night, before skidding to an abrupt halt.

"You OK?" said Mikey, pulling up beside his friend a moment later.

"Gordon flipping **Bennet**!" said Norm. "Yes, I'm OK. Just about!"

"Sorry, Norm," said Mikey.

"Should flipping think so too," muttered Norm.

"I'll take that as a 'no', then."

Norm stared at Mikey like a cat sizing up a mouse just before it pounces.

"Just checking," said Mikey quickly.

"Anyway, why are you so bothered about it?"

"What?" said Mikey.

"I didn't even know you **knew** Ellie," said Norm.

"Oh, there's lots you don't know about **me**, Norm," said Mikey mysteriously.

"Really?" said Norm doubtfully. "Such as?"

Mikey thought for a moment. "Actually, that's probably about it."

Norm sighed. "I know **one** thing."

"What?" said Mikey.

"You can be really flipping **annoying** sometimes, Mikey."

Mikey laughed.

"So?" said Norm.

"So what?" said Mikey.

"So, how come you know Ellie?"

Mikey pulled a face. "Well, she goes to the same *school* as us for a start!"

"Yeah, so?" said Norm. "So do *lots* of people. But you don't know *everybody*, you *doughnut*!"

"We have Food Technology together."

"Right," said Norm.

"Talking of doughnuts ..." said Mikey.

"What?" said Norm.

"We made scones yesterday," said Mikey.

Uh? thought Norm. What had **scones** got to do with **doughnuts**? And what had **any** of this got to do with Ellie?

"We made scones," said Mikey. "In Food Tech."

"Oh, right. I see."

"We were partners," said Mikey. "Me and Ellie."

"**Partners**?" said Norm.

"Not like **that**, Norm."

"Like what?" said Norm quickly.

"**That**!" said Mikey, his voice getting higher and higher. "Like we're getting **married** or something!"

"What are you on about, Mikey?"

"I'm not **old** enough to get married!"

"Uh?" said Norm. "Who said anything about you getting **married**?"

"I'm only **thirteen**, Norm!"

"I know how **old** you are, Mikey! Calm down! You look like you're going to blow a flipping fuse in a minute!"

Mikey looked at Norm for a moment. "What's she been telling you?"

"Who?" said Norm. "Ellie?"

Mikey nodded anxiously.

Norm shrugged. "Nothing."

"Nothing?" said Mikey.

"Yeah, **nothing**!" said Norm.

"Sure?"

"Gordon flipping **Bennet**, Mikey!" said Norm. "Of course I'm flipping sure!"

"OK," said Mikey.

"Why do you ask?"

Mikey shrugged. "Nothing."

"Nothing?"

Mikey nodded.

"So shut up then, you doughnut!"

"Sorry, Norm."

"What for?" said Norm.

"For acting all weird."

"Can't say I've noticed any difference," said Norm.

"Really?" said Mikey.

"Yeah," said Norm. "You're *always* flipping *weird*, Mikey."

Mikey looked relieved. Not that Norm noticed.

All **Norm** had noticed was that if they didn't get going soon, Mikey flipping **would** be old enough to get married.

"They turned out quite nicely, actually."

"Uh?" said Norm. "What did?"

"The scones," said Mikey.

Norm sighed. "Mikey?"

"Yeah?"

"Can you **please** stop talking about flipping **scones**? You're making me **hungry**!"

Mikey laughed. "You're **funny**, Norm."

"Don't **you** flipping start," said Norm.

"Start what?" said Mikey.

"Nothing," said Norm, starting to pedal off but then stopping again almost immediately.

"What's the matter?" said Mikey.

"I don't **believe** this," said Norm, getting off his bike and staring at the front wheel.

"What?" said Mikey.

"WHAT DO MEAN, **WHAT**?" wailed Norm. "I'VE GOT A FLIPPING **PUNCTURE**, MIKEY, THAT'S WHAT!"

"Aw, you're **kidding**!" said Mikey.

"Are **you** kidding?" said Norm, suddenly spinning round and glaring at Mikey.

"What?" said Mikey. "No, I asked **you** first, Norm."

"You asked me if I'm **kidding**?"

Mikey nodded.

"That I've got a **puncture**?"

Mikey nodded again.

"Why would I **joke** about having a puncture, Mikey?"

"Because you're ... funny?" said Mikey hesitantly.

Norm sighed. "Do I **look** like I'm flipping **kidding**, Mikey?"

Mikey studied Norm for a few seconds. "No, you don't."

"Look," said Norm, gesticulating towards the offending wheel.

"Oh, yeah," said Mikey. "It's as flat as a pancake."

"STOP GOING ON ABOUT FLIPPING **FOOD**!" yelled Norm.

"Sorry," said Mikey.

"Unbe-flipping-**lievable**," muttered Norm, turning back to his bike again.

"Bad luck, Norm."

Bad **luck**? thought Norm. Flipping **right** it was bad luck. Even by **his** standards. Because **no** one ever had worse luck than **Norm**. It sometimes felt like he'd been cursed by a flipping **witch** or some stupid **wizard** in one of those nerdy books that Brian read. **That's** how bad Norm's luck **normally** was. But

this? This took the flipping **biscuit**, this did. And not just some cheapo supermarket own-brand biscuit either. A proper **posh** biscuit from some posh shop that **only** sold flipping **biscuits**!

"You can't ride it like that," said Mikey.

"**Really**, Mikey?"

"Yeah, because if you do you could damage the ..." Mikey stopped for a second. "Oh, I see. You were being sarcastic."

But Norm wasn't actually listening any more. He was way too busy thinking just how monu-flipping-**mentally** unfair it was to have been **so** close to **finally** going biking in the woods, only to have it snatched away from him again at the last possible second. It was like something out of a nightmare. In fact, never mind **like** something out of a nightmare,

thought Norm. It **was** a flipping nightmare! An actual living, breathing flipping nightmare.

"Oh, well," said Mikey casually, setting off towards the woods. "See you later, Norm."

Norm stared, open mouthed, as his best friend disappeared around the corner. In fact, never mind open **mouthed** – Norm's jaw practically hit the ground as his best friend disappeared around the corner. How could Mikey **do** that? How could he even **think** about doing it? Just abandoning Norm in the middle of nowhere? Well, not exactly the middle of **nowhere**, but the middle of the shopping precinct. So the same thing really, as far as Norm was concerned. Mikey may as **well** have abandoned him **literally** in the middle of nowhere. Either way, thought Norm, it was

incredible. To just cycle off like that, leaving him stranded with a flat tyre.

What if it had been the other way round and **Mikey** had had a puncture? wondered Norm. Would **he** have just pedalled off like that and left **Mikey** standing there like a complete numpty? Well, yes, he probably would have done, thinking about it, thought Norm. But **that** wasn't the flipping point.

The point was that Mikey **had** actually done it. And it was **completely** out of flipping order.

"Sorry, Norm," said Mikey, suddenly reappearing.

"What?" said Norm, who'd been so lost in thought that he hadn't even **considered** the possibility that Mikey might actually change his mind and come back again. "Erm, oh, that's OK, Mikey. No hard feelings."

Mikey looked puzzled. "What? No, I just forgot to say something."

"Uh?" said Norm.

"I meant to say," said Mikey. "I love the video."

"What video?"

"The one of John and Brian dancing," said Mikey. "Brilliant!"

Norm sighed as he watched Mikey turn back around and disappear for the second time. Was it actually *possible* for a living, breathing nightmare to get any *worse*? Because if so, thought Norm, it just flipping *had*.

CHAPTER 12

Norm *still* couldn't quite believe what had just happened, as he walked all the way back home with his bike. He still couldn't quite believe what had just happened as he ate his lunch of own-brand baked beans on own-brand toast, washed down with a glass of own-brand milk, which for all Norm knew had come straight from an own-brand flipping *COW*. And he *still* couldn't quite believe what had just happened as he started to fix the

flat tyre. Not that he'd actually got very far with fixing it before Chelsea suddenly popped up on the other side of the fence as usual, like a particularly annoying meerkat.

"Hello, **Norman**!"

"Oh, **great**," muttered Norm under his breath.

"I'm fine, thanks. How are **you**?" said Chelsea.

Norm sighed. If he'd thought that being betrayed by his best friend was as bad as things could get today, he was obviously wrong.

"What are you **doing**?" said Chelsea.

"What does it **look** like I'm doing?" said Norm.

Chelsea looked for a moment. "Hmm, I'm not sure. Looks like you're fiddling about with your bike to **me**."

"Gordon flipping **Bennet**," mumbled Norm.

"Now, now, **Norman**," said Chelsea. "There's no need for **that**."

Norm sighed again. "You really want to know what I'm doing?"

Chelsea nodded. "I really want to know."

"You're not just going to take the mickey, or say something snarky?"

"As if," said Chelsea innocently.

"I'm taking the wheel off."

Chelsea pulled a face. "What are you doing **that** for?"

Norm sighed again. What did she flipping **think** he was doing it for? To see if he could ride his bike with just **one** wheel? If he'd wanted to do **that**, he'd have run off and joined a flipping **circus**!

"Come on, then," said Chelsea. "I'm on the edge of my seat here."

"Uh?" said Norm.

"Well, I mean I **would** be if I was actually sitting **down**."

"I'm fixing a puncture," said Norm. "And I thought you weren't going to say anything snarky?"

"I'm not being **snarky**," said Chelsea with a grin. "I'm genuinely fascinated to find out what you're doing."

Yeah, **right**, thought Norm, trying to loosen a

nut with a spanner. But so far it wasn't showing any signs of budging. And what definitely wasn't making it any **easier** was the fact that he now had a flipping audience. If one person could **be** described as an audience.

"So why are you doing **that**?" said Chelsea.

"What do you **mean**, why am I doing that?" said Norm, getting more and more wound up. "I just **told** you. 'Cos I've got a flipping **puncture**. And before you can fix a puncture you have to take the flipping **wheel** off!"

"All right**, Norman**!"
said Chelsea.
"Keep your hair on!"
She watched as
Norm continued to
do battle with the
stubborn nut.
"Looks quite hard."

"Yeah, it **is**, actually,"
said Norm, without
bothering to look up.

"So why don't you just buy a new one?"

"What?" said Norm irritably.

"Why don't you just buy a **new** one?" repeated Chelsea.

Norm pulled a face. "A new wheel, you mean?"

"No," said Chelsea. "A new **bike**."

Norm slowly turned to Chelsea, a look of utter disbelief on his face. "You're not **serious**, are you?"

"'Course I am," said Chelsea.

"You honestly think I should just go out and buy a new **bike**?"

"Well, that one's broken, isn't it?"

"What?" said Norm. "No. It's not actually **broken**."

"But you're having to **fix** it," said Chelsea.

"Yeah, I know, but ..."

"What?"

"That's what you **do**," said Norm. "Stuff goes wrong. You fix it."

Chelsea shrugged. "I just thought it might be easier to go and get a new one, that's all."

"That's **all**?"

"What's the problem, **Norman**?"

"What's the **problem**?" said Norm, as if Chelsea had just asked him what the point of **pizza** was.

"Yeah," said Chelsea.

"The ***problem***," said Norm, "is that a new bike would cost a hu-flipping-***mongous*** amount of money! And I don't ***have*** a hu-flipping-mongous amount of money!"

"Ah," said Chelsea. "That ***is*** a bit of a problem, isn't it?"

"What is?" said Dave, appearing at the front door and wandering over to see what Norm was doing.

"None of your flipping business, Dave!" spat Norm.

"Charming," said Dave.

"Hello, Dave," said Chelsea sweetly.

"Hello, Chelsea," said Dave. "How are you?"

"I'm ***very*** well, thank you for asking," said Chelsea, looking pointedly at Norm.

"Creep," said Norm to Dave.

"Why are you so horrible to your brothers, **Norman**?" said Chelsea.

"Yeah, why **are** you, **Norman**?" said Brian from the front door.

"And you can shut up, you little freak!" hissed Norm, swivelling round.

"Not **that** little, actually," said Brian.

"What?" said Norm.

"Dave's littler."

"Good point," said Dave. "I am."

"Hello, Chelsea, by the way," said Brian.

"Hello, Brian, by the way," said Chelsea with a grin.

"Have you heard Dave's impression of Norman?"

"No," said Chelsea. "But I'd **like** to."

"Gordon flipping **Bennet**," said Dave in his best Norm voice.

"That's **brilliant**!" laughed Chelsea.

"It's nothing **like** me," huffed Norm.

"How do **you** know, **Norman**?" said Chelsea.

Uh? thought Norm. What did she mean, how did **he** know?

"We never sound like we **think** we sound in our heads."

"Chelsea's right," said Brian. "We don't."

"Thank you, Brian," said Chelsea.

"You're **welcome**," said Brian.

"Love the video, by the way," said Chelsea. "Very funny!"

"Thanks," said Brian.

"I filmed that!" said Dave.

"It's got over a thousand likes!" said Chelsea.

"Whoa!" said Dave.

"**I know!**" said Chelsea. "Amazing, eh?"

Over a **thousand**? thought Norm. Actually, that **was** pretty amazing. But what was even **more** amazing was the fact that not so very long ago he hadn't been sure about whether to go to Ellie's or not that evening. And now he could hardly flipping **wait** to go. He still had no idea **why** he was going, or what he was going to do when he actually *got* there. But right now Norm couldn't care *less*. Because whatever it was, it *had* to be better than *this*. And even if it wasn't, at least he'd be somewhere

else. With no little brothers to constantly bug him and irritate him, like a couple of whining insects. And with nobody next door whose sole purpose in life appeared to be making *his* life as *miserable* and as *humiliating* as possible. And with no one doing stupid flipping impressions that sounded *nothing* like him whatso-flipping-*ever*!

"*Norman?*" said Chelsea.

"Sorry, what?" said Norm distractedly.

"I said, that's amazing, eh?"

"Yeah," said Norm with a nod. "Abso-flipping-*lutely*."

"Language," said Dave.

CHAPTER 13

The rest of the afternoon didn't exactly whoosh by in a *blur* as far as *Norm* was concerned. Much as he would have *liked* it to. But it passed by all the same, once Norm had finally given up on the idea of trying to fix his puncture. He obviously just wasn't *destined* to go biking. At least, not today anyway. Or yesterday for that matter. It was almost as if it had been written in the stars that he wasn't going to go. As if someone, somewhere was planning and controlling his every move. Not that Norm actually *believed* in destiny, or stuff being written in the flipping *stars*, of course. But that wasn't the point. The

point was that the afternoon *did* eventually pass. ***Without*** Norm having to invent some kind of time machine and pressing the fast-forward button. And before he knew it, he was standing outside Ellie's house, pressing the bell instead. At least, he ***hoped*** it was Ellie's house, anyway.

"Hi, Norman," said Ellie, opening the door a few moments later and wearing what, to Norm, looked like the kind of dress that a fairy godmother might have rejected on the grounds of it being just a bit ***too*** fancy. Not that Norm believed in fairy godmothers either, of course.

Ellie stood looking at Norm expectantly. But Norm didn't reply, opting instead to gawp like a gobsmacked goldfish.

"Aren't you going to say something?" said Ellie.

"You look ..." began Norm.

"Nice?" said Ellie.

"Different," said Norm.

"Thanks very **much**," said Ellie. "None taken!"

"What?"

"Don't you think I look **nice**, then?"

Gordon flipping **Bennet**, thought Norm. He hadn't been expecting **this** when he arrived. Not that he'd had the faintest idea **what** he'd been expecting when he arrived. But what was he supposed to say? Because nothing had ever prepared him for the situation that he now found himself in. Not that anything could have prepared Norm for **this**.

"Well?" said Ellie, hands on hips and posing like a model.

"Erm, yeah," said Norm.

"Yeah, what?" said Ellie.

"You **do** look nice?" said Norm hesitantly, unsure whether or not that was the correct answer.

"There," said Ellie. "**That** wasn't so difficult, was it?"

That's what **she** flipping thought, thought Norm. It was one of the most difficult things he'd ever had to do in his life. And that **included** the time he'd played the part of 'third tree from the left' in the school play.

"Anyway, I'm glad you think so," said Ellie. "Because I'm going out."

"What?" said Norm, a growing sense of dread beginning to bubble and boil away inside him like water in a kettle. So ***that's*** why she was dressed up! She was going out. But where to? And, more importantly, who with?

"I'm going out," said Ellie again. "Or rather, ***we're*** going out."

Norm stared at Ellie, goggle-eyed and speechless. She hadn't ***really*** just said what he ***thought*** she'd just said, had she? She was asking him out? Well, not ***asking*** him. ***Telling*** him! And all because he supposedly 'owed' her a flipping favour? All because he'd scratched her back? Or she'd scratched ***his***? Norm couldn't

quite remember which way round it was now. But that wasn't the flipping point. The point was that it looked like it was payback time. Because *that* was the way the flipping cookie *crumbled*! This wasn't just a *nightmare*. This was like *all* the flipping nightmares Norm had ever had rolled into one whacking great *big* nightmare the size of a flipping great big nightmarish *bus*!

"Not *all* of us, obviously," said Ellie, after what seemed to Norm like an *eternity* but which, in reality, was probably no more than a couple of seconds.

"What?" croaked Norm, finally regaining the power of speech.

"Just me and my parents," said Ellie. "Not Santa."

Wait a minute, thought Norm. So she **wasn't** asking him out after all? Halle-flipping-**lujah**! But in that case, why was he even **here**? Why had Ellie asked him round? It just didn't make sense! But then, thought Norm, nothing ever flipping **did**.

WOOF! WOOF! WOOF! went Santa, suddenly bounding into view and very nearly knocking Ellie her off her feet.

"Yes, I **know** you want to go to the Salsa Night," said Ellie, bending over and stroking the dog. "But you **can't**, can you? No, you can't."

"Salsa Night?" said Norm.

"Of **course**," said Ellie. "The one at school. Where did you **think** I was going?"

"Dunno," said Norm. "A fancy-dress party?"

"Charming," said Ellie.

"That's where my mum and dad are going," said Norm. "The salsa night. Not a fancy-dress party."

Ellie laughed. "You **are** funny, Norman."

Norm looked at Ellie. "So, er ..."

"Oh, yes, sorry, I almost forgot," said Ellie. "I need you to baby-sit."

Norm pulled a face. "**Baby**-sit?"

"Well, not **baby**-sit," said Ellie. "**Doggy**-sit."

"Uh?" said Norm.

"You don't **like** being left on your own, do you, Santa?" said Ellie, giving the dog another stroke. "No, you **don't**!"

"So …" began Norm.

"What?" said Ellie.

"Is *that* what the favour is?"

"Well, of *course*. You were the obvious choice!"

WOOF! WOOF! went Santa, wagging his tail furiously.

"Yes, I *know* you love Norman," said Ellie. "Yes, I *do*!"

Norm puffed out his cheeks and breathed a massive sigh of relief. Because at that precise moment in time, the feeling was entirely mutual. *He* genuinely loved *Santa*! And compared to  the prospect of having to go to some stupid so-called *salsa night* with Ellie and being forced to watch his parents, so-called *dancing* together like a pair of snakes, spending a couple of hours with him was going to be like a stroll in the flipping park! Though why anyone would ever want to actually **stroll** in a park when you could go biking in a park instead was a mystery to Norm. But that was another matter entirely.

"Why?" said Ellie, looking up at Norm. "What did you **think** I was going to ask you?"

"Er, nothing," said Norm quickly.

"Nothing?"

"I didn't know **what** you were going to ask," said Norm, desperately wishing that Ellie would just hurry up and flipping go now.

"Why have you gone red?" said Ellie.

"What?" said Norm. "I haven't."

"Oh, hello, Norman," said Ellie's mum, appearing in the hallway. "I thought you were Mikey!"

What? thought Norm. Why would she think *that*? And what would Mikey be doing turning up at Ellie's house on a Saturday night, anyway?

"Didn't you *know* that Ellie and Mikey were going to the salsa night together?" said Ellie's mum, as if she'd read Norm's mind.

"What?" said Norm. "I mean, pardon? I mean, no. I didn't, actually."

"I think she *likes* him," whispered Ellie's mum.

"No, I *don't*, Mum!" protested Ellie. "Not like *that*! We're just going to *dance* together, that's all!"

Of **course**! thought Norm. That must have been what Mikey had had to go home and **practise** yesterday! Salsa dancing! Because his mum and dad knew how to do it! Why hadn't he thought of that before? Then again, thought Norm, why on earth **would** he have thought of that before? There was no reason whatso-flipping-**ever** why Norm would have suspected that **that** was what Mikey had been doing!

"Anyway, I'm meeting him at school," said Ellie.

"Well, we'd better hurry up then, hadn't we?" said Ellie's mum, bustling away again. "We don't want to be late!"

"You're not **bothered**, are you?" said Ellie, turning back to Norm.

Norm pulled a face. "Bothered? Why would I be **bothered**?"

Ellie shrugged. "I don't know. I just thought you might be, that's all."

Norm thought for a moment. Not only was he

not flipping bothered, he was anything ***but*** flipping bothered. He was the complete polar ***opposite*** of flipping bothered. Whatever ***that*** was. ***Un-***flipping-bothered? Who cared? thought Norm. Because in an instant, he'd totally forgiven Mikey for leaving him with a puncture earlier on that day. ***And*** for not being able to go biking the ***previous*** day. Because if ***Mikey*** was going to the Salsa  Night with Ellie, it meant that ***he*** flipping ***wasn't***! And for that reason alone, Norm would ***always*** be grateful to Mikey. No wonder he'd been acting all weird, though. He just probably didn't want Norm to ***know*** what he was doing! And, frankly, thought Norm, who could flipping ***blame*** him? Because if it had been the other way round, ***he*** definitely wouldn't have told ***Mikey***!

"Oh, well," said Ellie, standing to one side. "You'd better come in."

Yeah, thought Norm, walking past her. He better flipping had. Before she changed her *mind*.

"What's your favourite kind of biscuit, Norman?"

"Jammie Dodgers," said Norm, without a moment's hesitation.

"Jammie Dodgers, eh?" said Ellie, leading Norm towards the kitchen. "This could be your lucky day!"

First time for flipping *everything*, thought Norm, following on behind.

CHAPTER 14

The smell hit Norm the second he got back home. Not the vaguely rotten, fishy, unwashed aroma of his brothers, which was the smell that normally assaulted Norm's nostrils as he opened the front door. And not the smell of stinky Cockapoo, either. Not even the overpowering stench of his dad's beloved prehistoric aftershave, **_Beast Pour Homme_**, because his parents still hadn't arrived back yet.

No, the smell that greeted Norm like an old friend was the unmistakable whiff of fresh, warm pizza dough, instantly making 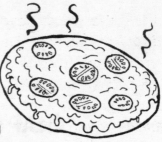 him drool like a waterfall, despite the fact that he'd spent most of the evening at Ellie's house stuffing his face with as many Jammie Dodgers as he could manage. Which turned out to be quite a lot, as it happened. Twenty-eight, to be precise. Not all at once, obviously. Although Norm probably **would** have done if he **could** have done. And not that he was counting, anyway. And not only **that**, but they weren't even supermarket own-brand Jammie Dodgers like he was **used** to eating. They were **proper** Jammie Dodgers! So despite the doggy-sitting technically being a **favour** and therefore Norm not actually being **paid** to do it, he definitely felt like he was getting the better part of the so-called **deal**.

But then he would have felt that anyway, even **without** the Jammie Dodgers. Because at least Norm had been spared the complete and utter humiliation of having to go to the so-called flipping Salsa Night and witnessing his parents' so-called **dancing**! Even **better**, he'd been spared the trauma of having to dance with Ellie. It didn't even bother Norm that, according to Ellie, Mikey had been really **amazing** at salsa. Because at least it hadn't been **him**!

Wait a flipping minute, thought Norm, stepping into the hall and closing the front door behind him. How come he could smell **pizza**? Not that there was anything **wrong** with the smell of pizza, of course. Far from it. It was the best smell in the world. The problem was, they hadn't actually **had** pizza for tea, before he'd left to go to Ellie's! His mum had cooked some strange-looking – and even stranger **tasting** – concoction that looked more like it had come straight from a flipping

laboratory rather than out of the flipping **oven**. There'd been **vegetables** and all kinds of weird stuff in it. Norm didn't know exactly what. And he was pretty sure he didn't **want** to know exactly what, either. What Norm **wanted** to know, exactly, was how come **pizza** had been consumed in his absence? And it definitely **had** been consumed. Because Norm could sniff out pizza like an anteater sniffing out ants. And it just wasn't flipping on, as far as Norm was concerned. How **could** they? Just wait for him to leave and then eat, all over **again**?

Because that's what Grandpa and his conniving, evil little brothers had clearly done. And it wasn't just out-flipping-**rageous**. It was inhumane.

236

"Ah, **there** you are," said Grandpa as Norm poked his nose into the kitchen, closely followed by the rest of him.

"How's your **girlfriend**, Norman?" Brian grinned.

"I **told** you, Brian," whispered Dave. "Ellie's not Norman's **girlfriend**! He doesn't actually **have** a girlfriend!"

"Oh, right," said Brian.

But it didn't matter. And Dave didn't even need to **whisper**. He could have shouted through a loudhailer.

Because Norm wasn't listening, **anyway**. He'd just spotted the very **last** thing he wanted to spot. A pile of flipping **takeaway** pizza boxes on the table in front of where Grandpa and his brothers were sitting. As if it wasn't bad enough already, thought Norm. Because they **could** have just grabbed some supermarket own-brand pizzas from the freezer. But, oh no. They just **had** to get flipping **takeaways**, didn't they? And then suddenly it got even **worse**. Because – and as if to rub even **more** salt into the wound and generally make him feel even **more** rubbish than he was already – Norm spotted the all too familiar-looking logos printed **on** the pizza boxes.

"What's the matter, Norman?" said Grandpa. "You look like someone just peed in your packed lunch."

"EURGH!" went Brian and Dave together, screwing up their faces in disgust.

"But ..." began Norm.

"What?" said Grandpa.

"You got **takeaway** pizzas?"

"We certainly did," said Grandpa.

"FROM WIKIPIZZA?" wailed Norm, like a wildebeest about to give birth.

"No poop, Poirot," said Grandpa.

"Uh?" said Norm.

"So you can read, then?" said Grandpa. "Excellent."

"Poirot's a detective," explained Brian. "Well, a **fictional** detective, anyway."

"What?" said Norm.

"He's made up," said Brian. "He's just a character in a book."

Norm sighed. He was beginning to feel like **he** was a character in a flipping book, too. And so far it had been a really **rubbish** book. But was there going to be a happy ending? That's what **Norm** wanted to know.

"Anyway, technically it wasn't a takeaway," said Brian.

Norm pulled a face.

"We didn't actually **collect** it," said Brian. "It was delivered."

"By a guy on a moped," added Dave. "It was really cool."

But Norm didn't care **how** the pizza had been delivered. It could have been delivered by an alien on a space hopper as far as he was concerned. What Norm was **far** more bothered about was **where** the pizzas had actually been delivered **from**.

"You seem surprised, Norman?" said Grandpa.

Surprised? thought Norm. That he'd been the victim of such a monstrous miscarriage of justice? That his jammy little brothers had been gorging on the finest pizza on the planet – and possibly in the entire flipping ***universe*** – whilst ***he'd*** been just around the flipping corner, ***doggy***-sitting and eating biscuits? That, once again, it had been proved beyond ***any*** shadow of a flipping ***doubt*** that ***everything*** was just ***so*** flipping ***unfair***? No, thought Norm. Thinking about it, he wasn't in the ***least*** bit surprised. It was what he'd come to expect.

"I just thought Brian and Dave deserved a bit of a treat, that's all," said Grandpa.

"A ***treat***?" said Norm. "What for?"

"Well, for not being allowed to go to the salsa night,

of course," said Grandpa, as if it was a screamingly obvious answer to a screamingly stupid question.

No way, thought Norm. His brothers had actually been **rewarded**, for **that**? For **not** being mentally scarred for the rest of their lives and for potentially saving thousands of pounds in psychiatrists' fees? They'd never know just how flipping **lucky** they were that they **didn't** go and have to watch their parents prancing about like prize doughnuts!

"Talking of salsa," said Grandpa.

"What?" said Norm.

"I enjoyed the video."

"You mean ... ?"

Grandpa nodded. "The one of Brian and John dancing. Yes."

"We showed it to Grandpa, didn't we, Grandpa?" said Dave.

"You certainly did," said Grandpa. "And very funny it was too."

Gordon flipping **Bennet**, thought Norm. Was there anybody who *hadn't* seen the flipping video yet? An undiscovered tribe of monkey-juggling native Indians in the Amazonian rain forest, perhaps?

"Over eighteen hundred likes, so far," said Brian,  as if he'd been reading Norm's mind.

"Grandpa said we should send it somewhere," said Dave.

Norm looked at Dave. "What do you mean, send it somewhere?"

"You know," said Dave. "To one of those TV programmes that show funny clips and pranks and stuff."

Norm shrugged. "What would we want to do **that** for?"

"Seriously?" said Dave.

"Seriously," said Norm.

Dave stared at his eldest brother for a moment, as if he couldn't quite believe that he was having to spell it out. As if their normal roles had temporarily been reversed and **he** was nearly twice as old as **Norm** was. "For the money?"

"What?" said Norm.

"For the money," repeated Dave, raising his eyebrows.

"Duh," said Brian.

"I agree with Brian," said Grandpa.

"What?" said Norm.

"Duh," said Grandpa.

Norm thought for a moment. Actually, that wasn't

such a bad idea. In fact, **_thinking_** about it, it was an abso-flipping-lutely **_brilliant_** idea. If the video **_did_** get shown, then maybe he'd be able to do what Chelsea had suggested and buy a whole new bike, instead of constantly having to fiddle about and fix the one he'd already got! It was genius! Why hadn't he thought of that before?

"Of course, you'd have to split the money between you," said Grandpa.

"What?" said Norm, as if he hadn't even **_thought_** of that. Which he hadn't.

"You'd have to split the money three ways," said Grandpa. "It's only fair."

Fair? thought Norm. What was fair about **_that_**? He'd sooner split **_himself_** three ways than split any money he might get with his flipping **_brothers_**.

"Yeah," said Brian. "It's **me** in the video!"

"And it was **me** who actually **filmed** it," said Dave.

"Yeah," said Norm. "On **my** flipping iPad! Without **my** flipping permission!"

"So?" said Brian and Dave together.

Norm sighed wearily. He didn't even know why he bothered arguing sometimes. Or **any** time for that matter. What was the flipping **point**? Nothing **ever** went his way. Even when he thought it was **about** to. Something **always** flipping happened. Always flipping **had** done. Always flipping **would** do. Because **that** was the way that Norm's flipping own-brand cookie **crumbled**!

"We're home!" said Norm's mum, suddenly walking into the kitchen.

Obviously, thought Norm. Where did his mum **think** they thought she was? Still at the flipping Salsa Night?

"Are you two still up?" said Norm's dad, appearing next to Norm's mum and eyeballing Brian and Dave.

Obviously, thought Norm again. What did his dad **think** he was looking at? A flipping hologram?

"My fault," said Grandpa, his eyes crinkling ever so slightly in the corners. "We've been having fun, haven't we, boys?"

"YEAH!" said Brian and Dave together.

"Up to bed now, both of you," said Norm's mum. "And don't forget to brush your teeth!"

"'Kay, Mum," said Brian, getting up and heading for the stairs. "Night, Grandpa!"

"Night, night," said Grandpa.

"Night, Grandpa," said Dave, giving Grandpa a hug. "Thanks for the pizza."

"You're welcome," said Grandpa, ruffling Dave's hair before sending him on his way with a friendly pat on the backside.

"Talking about not forgetting," said Norm's dad to Norm, once both his brothers had gone.

"What?" said Norm.

"You may well ask," said his dad.

He just flipping **had**, thought Norm.

"We were talking to Ellie, at the salsa night," said Norm's mum.

"Right," said Norm.

"What a lovely couple she and Mikey make, by the way. And I had no *idea* Mikey was such a good dancer!"

Whatever, thought Norm.

"Anyway," said Norm's dad impatiently.

Yeah, anyway? thought Norm.

"She told us about the homework," said Norm's mum.

Norm pulled a face. "Uh?"

"The geography homework?"

"Oh, *that* homework," said Norm, as if he'd only just remembered. Which he had.

"Yes," said Norm's dad. "*That* homework. The homework you'll be doing first thing tomorrow morning."

 blurted Norm.

"That's the deal," said his dad. "No homework, no biking. Simple."

"You **do** actually want to **go** biking, don't you, love?" said Norm's mum.

"Uh?" said Norm. "Of **course** I do, Mum!"

"Well, then," said Norm's mum. "You'd better get cracking, hadn't you?"

"Gordon flipping **Bennet**," muttered Norm.

"What was that?" said his dad.

"Nothing," said Norm, heading for the stairs.

THE END

WANT MORE

NORM?

Read on for a hilarious
extract from
MAY CAUSE IRRITATION

CHAPTER 1

Norm knew it was going to be one of those days when he woke up and found himself standing at a supermarket checkout, totally naked.

"I'm afraid that's not allowed," said the checkout assistant.

"Pardon?" said Norm.

"It's strictly against the rules," said the assistant.

"What is?" said Norm. "Shopping without any clothes on?"

"No," said the assistant. "Having ten items in your basket. This checkout's nine items or less."

Norm did a quick count. Sure enough, there were ten items in the basket – every one of them the supermarket's own, cheaper brand.

"Sorry, I'll put one back," said Norm.

"It's too late for that," said the assistant.

"What?" said Norm, with a growing sense of disbelief.

"It's too late. I'm going to have to ask you to leave."

"Are you serious?" said Norm.

As if to demonstrate just how serious she was, the checkout assistant pushed a button and spoke into a microphone. "Security to checkout three, please – security to checkout three."

"But..." said Norm.

"Stand away from the till," said a strangely familiar sounding voice. "You have ten seconds to comply."

You have Ten seconds to COMPLY

Norm turned round to see a strangely familiar looking security guard approaching. "Dad? It's me! Norman!"

But Norm's dad took no notice. "Here, take this," he said, handing Norm a packet of own-brand coco pops and ushering him towards the exit.

"It's OK thanks, I'm not hungry," said Norm.

"Not to eat," said Norm's dad. "To cover up your..."

"Oh, right," said Norm, suddenly remembering he was butt naked.

What was going on? wondered Norm. And why was his dad dressed as a security guard? Was he going to a fancy dress party? If so then a security guard at a supermarket was a pretty rubbish thing to go as. Unless, of course, the theme of the party was supermarkets. Or security guards. And frankly neither seemed terribly likely.

"This way please," said Norm's dad officiously.

Cameras flashed as Norm was led from the store wearing nothing but a strategically placed packet of own-brand coco pops. A crowd had gathered to watch the unfolding drama and in the distance the wail of a police siren could be heard, getting louder and louder.

"All right, **Norman**?" said another strangely familiar sounding voice.

Norm looked round to see Chelsea, his occasional next-door neighbour, grinning from ear to ear. Worse still, she appeared to be filming proceedings with her phone. If things could actually *get* any more humiliating, they just *had*.

"I see you've only got a small packet," laughed Chelsea.

Norm could feel himself blushing.

"How could you do this to us, Norman?" said yet another familiar sounding voice.

It was Norm's mum. Next to her, Norm could see his middle brother, Brian, and next to Brian his youngest brother, Dave.

"You've brought shame on the whole family," said Norm's mum, gravely.

"No he hasn't," chirped Dave. "This is well funny, this is!"

"Shut up, Dave!" said Brian.

"Honestly, love, this is very embarrassing," said Norm's mum.

"It's not my fault, Mum!" protested Norm. "I didn't see any signs saying 'No naked shopping allowed'!"

"What?" said Norm's mum. "No, I meant it's very embarrassing you shopping in a place like this. We normally go to Tesco's. What on earth will the neighbours think?"

"Your mother's right, Norman," said Norm's dad. "Surely things aren't *that* bad, are they?"

Norm looked at his dad for a second. If it wasn't for him getting flipping sacked, none of this would have happened in the first flipping place.

"I dunno, Dad. *You* tell *me!*"

But before Norm's dad could reply, a police car screeched to a halt and a dog got out of the driver's door.

"You're under arrest on suspicion of having ten items at the nine items or less checkout," said the dog. "You have the right to remain silent. Anything you say may be taken down and used as evidence against you."

Norm chose to remain silent. The truth was Norm couldn't have said anything if he'd wanted to. He'd started to feel a bit woozy and light-headed. Like he was about to faint. Whether it was the shock of seeing a dog driving a police car, or a dog that could *talk* driving a police car, was hard to say.

"Norman?" said Norm's mum, as Norm's legs suddenly turned to jelly and he collapsed in a quivering heap on the floor.

CHAPTER 2

"Norman?" said Norm's mum again. "Time to wake up, love."

Norm grunted.

"Rise and shine," said Norm's mum, shaking Norm gently by the shoulder.

Norm still showed no sign of waking up.

"Time to get dressed."

That did the trick. Norm sat up in a flash.

"Where's my coco pops?" he said, thrashing about the bedclothes in a panic.

"What?" said his mum.

"The packet of coco pops!" said Norm. "I need it!"

"What for?"

Norm looked down and was mightily relieved to see that he was wearing pyjamas.

"Er, nothing."

"I think *someone's* been having a dream!" laughed Norm's mum.

Norm looked around him. Mountain-biking posters on the walls? Check. Pile of mountain-biking magazines on his bedside table? Check. Mountain-biking helmet hanging behind the door? Check.

"Is ***this*** a dream, Mum?"

"Pardon?"

"Is this a dream?" said Norm. "Maybe I'm ***dreaming*** that I'm dreaming."

Norm's mum smiled.

"Maybe *you're* dreaming, Mum," said Norm. "Maybe *I'm* in *your* dream! Maybe none of this is real."

"Or maybe you should just get up," said Norm's mum. "It's nearly ten o'clock!"

"I thought it was Saturday," said Norm.

"It is."

"So why do I have to get up?"

"Your cousins are coming, remember?"

"Aw, no!" wailed Norm.

Now Norm knew for sure this wasn't a dream. It was an

absolute-flipping-nightmare!

His cousins? His perfect flipping cousins? What did they have to come and ruin everything for?

"How long are they staying?"

"All day," said Norm's mum. "We're having lunch and then we're all going for a walk."

A **walk**? thought Norm. If there was one thing worse than spending time with his perfect cousins it was being forced to go on a flipping walk with them! Norm couldn't see the point of walks at the best of times. He did quite enough walking without ever actually *going* on one.
He **walked** to school.

He **walked** up and down the stairs.

He'd even been known to **walk** to the TV to change channels if he couldn't find the remote and his brothers weren't around to do it for him.

Walking was something you did to get from A to B in the shortest possible time, by the shortest possible route. Walking was most definitely *not* something you did for pleasure!

"You're not serious, Mum? A **walk**?"

"What's wrong with that, Norman?"

"What's *right* with it, you mean!"

"Now, now, don't be like that."

Norm had a thought. There was one way of making the experience at least vaguely bearable.

"Can I bring my bike?"

"No, you can't bring your bike! We're going on a *walk*!"

Norm sighed with resignation. Short of being struck down by an incurable tropical disease, he knew that there was very little chance of getting out of this.

"Oh, come on, Norman," said Norm's mum. "They're not that bad, are they?"

Bad? thought Norm. His cousins were worse than bad, with their perfect teeth and their perfect hair and their perfect manners. Always banging on about playing some random instrument in some stupid concert, or going to some country Norm had never even heard of. *They* hadn't had to move to a smaller house because they were skint! If *they'd* been forced to eat own-brand coco pops they'd have been straight on the phone to flipping Childline!

"Oh, and open the window before you come down, love," said Norm's mum, disappearing through the doorway. "It smells awful in here."

"Yeah, so?" muttered Norm under his breath.

"Your cousins are coming!" said Norm's mum, whose hearing was a lot better than Norm thought it was.

"And I suppose ***they*** never fart," said Norm.

"Just do it please, love," shouted Norm's mum.

Norm grudgingly got out of bed and opened the window. Knowing his perfect cousins, they probably ***didn't*** fart. And even if they ***did***, they probably smelt of flipping flowers or something.

Norm glanced outside. It looked like it was about to pee it down with rain. The sky was the colour of...of...actually, Norm couldn't think what the sky was the colour of. No doubt his perfect cousins would be able to though. In fact, knowing his perfect cousins they'd probably write a flipping poem about it. Without even being told to!

Flipping freaks of nature, thought Norm, trudging wearily towards the stairs.

Read **MAY CAUSE IRRITATION** to find out what happens next!

NORM WILL RETURN IN ...

THE WORLD OF NORM

MAY BE RECYCLED

Don't miss his **ELEVENTH**
laugh-out-loud adventure!

THE WORLD OF
NORM
MAY CONTAIN PRIZES

HELLO, NORM FANS. DO YOU WANT TO WIN A BRAND-NEW BIKE? YES, THAT'S RIGHT. A BRAND-NEW, SHINY BIKE!

- Go to the World of Norm website at: www.worldofnorm.co.uk

- Enter the competition

- You may win a prize!

BLING!

Closing date: 31/07/2016

See website for full terms and conditions.

ORCHARD BOOKS

Illustrations © Donough O'Malley